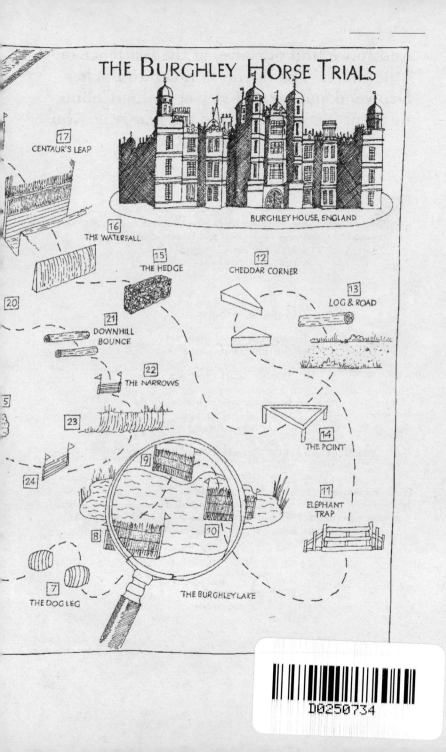

And so we find ourselves at the last fence on
the course. Thank you so much to Rachel
Denwood and Lizzie Ryley at HarperCollins,
my agent Nancy Miles and the real Issie, who
has been with me all the way.

www.stacygregg.co.uk

First published in Great Britain by HarperCollins Children's Books in 2010
HarperCollins Children's Books is a division of HarperCollinsPublishers Ltd
1 London Bridge Street, London SE1 9GF
This edition published in 2016

24

www.harpercollins.co.uk

Text copyright © Stacy Gregg, 2011
Illustrations © Fiona Land 2011

ISBN: 978-0-00-729932-4

Printed and bound by CPI Group (UK) Ltd, Croydon, CR0 4YY

MIX
Paper from
responsible sources
FSC C007454

Nightstorm and the Grand Slam

In the glamorous and dangerous world of three-day eventing there are three super-elite competitions that together are regarded above all the rest as the very greatest test of a rider's skill and courage.

These three events are: The Kentucky Four-Star, The Badminton Horse Trials and The Burghley Horse Trials.

Winning any one of these famous equestrian contests is considered a remarkable feat. Even more incredible, however, is the rider who can win all of them in a clean sweep. This three-in-a-row victory is, without a doubt, the most coveted title in the world of eventing: a phenomenon known simply as the Grand Slam.

CHAPTER 1

It was day one of the Badminton Horse Trials. The first crucial phase of the three-day event was underway and throughout the morning, one after another, elite combinations of horse and rider had performed their dressage tests with precision and elegance as the crowds in the grandstand looked on.

The sun was high in the sky by the time the final competitor rode into the main stadium. Like the other riders before her, she was dressed in a long black tailcoat and a silk topper. Underneath the top hat, her startlingly youthful face was fixed in a serious expression as she took her last warm-up lap, cantering her magnificent bay horse around the perimeter of the arena.

"Ladies and gentlemen," commentator Mike Partridge began his introduction, "our last rider of the day is only seventeen years old and this is her first time here at the Badminton Horse Trials. However, do not dismiss this young equestrienne just because of her age. Two weeks ago this talented girl rode at the prestigious international Kentucky Four-Star in Lexington, USA and took home the winner's medal in an astonishing performance on a horse that she had ridden for the first time just two days before!"

Mike Partridge's voice shrank to a whisper as he watched the rider on the bay stallion line up ready to begin her test.

"We have already seen her in the arena this morning, putting in a very good performance on Victory, the Australian-bred gelding owned by Mrs Tulia Disbrowe. This is her second ride of the day, on her own horse this time…" Mike Partridge paused for dramatic effect, "…ladies and gentlemen, this is Isadora Brown riding Nightstorm!"

As she cantered down the centre line, Issie tried to keep her composure. To the crowds in the stands she might have looked calm and collected, but beneath the heavy tailcoat her shirt was soaked with sweat. She was exhausted and shaken, having just spent the past hour in a heated battle of wills in the warm-up arena with Nightstorm – a fight that had ended emphatically when the stallion finally threw a massive hissy fit and bucked her off!

"Easy boy," she murmured as they halted. "Please don't lose it again, not now…"

Storm was the most talented horse she'd ever ridden – but the counterbalance to his genius was a hot temper which surfaced at moments like this one. She'd been trying to practise their flying changes when Storm had decided he'd had enough of this dressage stuff. Putting in a swift and violent buck, he'd taken Issie totally by surprise, and before she knew what was happening the ground was rushing up to meet her.

The sand of the arena made for a soft landing and there was no damage done – apart from a slight dent to her top hat. Still, it was the last thing her nerves needed right before going in to perform her test and as she dusted herself off and mounted up to enter the arena she felt very rattled indeed.

As she saluted the judges and cast a glance around

the crowded stands of the main stadium, she hoped that Storm had got it out of his system. If he threw her again here in the arena – with thousands of eyes upon her and everything they'd worked for on the line – it would be another matter entirely.

Urging Storm forward into an extended trot, she had a sick sensation in her belly. They were about to cross the centre of the arena and execute the first of three flying changes. This was the moment of truth! Would Storm fight her again, in front of everyone?

Bracing herself for the worst, Issie put her legs on and asked the stallion to perform the first change. There was a moment of terror when Storm swished his tail – but he didn't buck. He changed legs perfectly at her command and Issie felt a wave of confidence surge through her. Storm was on her side and he was moving magnificently as she urged him on through two more flying changes and then came down the long side of the arena in a graceful extended canter.

"My word!" Mike Partridge sounded frightfully impressed. "A stunning extended canter – just look at the paces on this young horse!"

In the arena, Storm was performing a half-pass,

crossing his legs like a ballerina. The stallion seemed to float above the ground, neck arched in submission, muscles and sinews flexing and trembling as he carried himself across the sand surface.

"Nightstorm has the most remarkable bloodlines for an eventer," Mike Partridge continued. "He was bred from Isadora's pony-club mare – a chestnut Anglo-Arab named Blaze. Nightstorm's sire was the great Marius, one of the legendary horses of the performing Andalusian troupe – El Caballo Danza Magnifico – and certainly you can see from the way this young stallion moves that he has inherited his father's incredible movement and grace."

As Mike Partridge was speaking, the bay stallion flew through the last flying change, and then cantered once more up the centre line to complete the final manoeuvre of the dressage test.

Issie halted the horse square, saluting in three directions to the judges who were placed around the sides of the arena, and then, dropping her reins, she bent down over her horse's neck with a huge grin covering her face and gave him a massive, slappy pat.

"And she has every reason to be happy with that!"

Mike Partridge enthused. "That superb test will put her right up there on the leaderboard!"

As she exited the arena to the applause of the crowd, Issie was shaking from the adrenalin rush of performing. At the start of her test she had been genuinely worried that she might be publicly dumped to the ground by her temperamental, difficult horse. Instead, Storm had shocked her completely by delivering his best-ever dressage performance!

Outside of the arena and out of view of the crowds, Issie threw her arms around Storm's neck, able to give him a proper hug at last.

"You are a super-clever boy!" she said proudly.

"Don't give him all the credit!"

Issie turned around to see Tom Avery smiling at her.

"You deserve the lion's share of the praise," Avery insisted. "It was your riding that saved the day in there. Storm was on a hair trigger the whole time but you handled him perfectly."

Issie brushed off the compliment. "He's not trying to be naughty, Tom, he's just got too much energy."

"Well, he'll need all of it tomorrow," Avery said. "That

cross-country course is over six kilometres long."

Badminton's infamous cross-country phase was considered to be the most difficult four-star track in the world. For the riders who survived and made it all the way round, the showjumping would follow the day after. It would take a clear round in both of these disciplines, as well as an excellent dressage test score, to bring home the coveted trophy.

Despite her stellar performance at Kentucky, Issie was far from the favourite to claim glory here at this prestigious British horse trials.

Her win in the States had been put down to good fortune. Valmont Liberty was an eventing superstar and there were some on the eventing circuit who speculated that Issie had been handed a gift when she was given the last-minute chance to ride on a push-button mount.

In reality Liberty was far from easy to handle and her win at Kentucky had been hard-fought. But clearly the bookies believed that Issie was a one-hit wonder and had put her odds of winning at 50-1.

There was no chance of Issie repeating her dream ride with Liberty here. Kentucky was only two weeks before

Badminton, which made it impossible to ride the same horse at both events as you couldn't transport a horse from the USA to England with enough recovery time to compete.

But Issie had never planned to ride Liberty, or her other Kentucky mount, Comet, at Badminton. Her plan had always been to keep two of her best horses back in England. Nightstorm and Victory had both been chosen over a year ago as her Badminton rides.

Victory had been an unexpected but very welcome addition, not long after they'd moved to England and set up their stables at The Laurels, a farm in the heart of Wiltshire.

Issie knew Victory from long ago. She had once ridden the athletic brown Thoroughbred at the Pony Club Express Eventing competition in Melbourne, Australia. Then, out of the blue, Victory's owner Tulia Disbrowe got in touch to ask if Issie wanted to take over the ride on her horse.

"Victory's rider had a bad fall at the Adelaide four-star," Tulia explained over the phone from Australia. "He's fractured his back so he's out for the rest of the season. I've trialled several other jockeys but none of them really clicked – and then I thought of you. I hear you're setting up training stables with Tom Avery and Francoise and I was wondering if you'd like to take the horse to England with you."

Issie couldn't believe it. Over the years since she'd last ridden him, Victory had become an experienced advanced eventer. He was competing at four-star – the very top level. And Tulia was offering to sponsor him to the UK so that Issie could ride him!

One foggy morning in December, Avery, Issie and Francoise met Victory off the flight from Melbourne at Heathrow, and after the gelding had been through quarantine they took him home to The Laurels where he settled in as if he had been there all his life.

When the eventing season got underway a couple of months later, Issie began riding Victory on the circuit. It didn't take long to rebuild their bond and by the following October they were in good enough form to place third at the prestigious Boekelo horse trials in the Netherlands.

By the season's end, both Victory and Storm had clearly marked themselves out as the stars of The Laurels' stables. When the call for entries for the Badminton

Horse Trials rolled around, there was no doubt in Issie's mind that they were the ones she wanted to ride.

Entering two horses was common practice at Badminton. However, Issie had her work cut out adapting her riding style between them.

Victory was a typical Thoroughbred – catlike and elegant with lean limbs and a gallop that swallowed the ground on a cross-country course – Nightstorm was burly and heavy-set with the strong haunches and powerful neck that spoke of his Andalusian bloodlines.

But it wasn't just their physiques that were opposite. Their personalities were also worlds apart.

"When you ride Victory, you ride with your head," Francoise once said. "Nightstorm is different – he must be ridden with your heart."

The French dressage trainer was right. To get the best out of Storm, Issie needed more than technical perfection – she needed to emotionally connect with the stallion; to convince him that he wanted this as much as she did.

It wasn't easy. Storm had a mind of his own – as he had proven today in the warm-up arena! Even as a young colt he had been headstrong, and now that the stallion was fully grown he had become even harder for Issie to manage. Issie would often end a schooling session frustrated by the power struggle between her and the obstinate bay stallion. She would have given up on him entirely if Storm weren't so ridiculously talented. His dressage paces were elevated and spectacular, his jumping ability was unrivalled, and despite his burly conformation he was speedy and agile across country. He was the perfect eventer. Or at least he would have been if it weren't for his unpredictable dressage antics. At the Boekelo horse trials, he had thrown what could only be called a tantrum – kicking out his hindquarters in a dramatic buck every time Issie asked him to change his paces. Issie had stayed onboard but she had left the arena almost in tears.

"Storm's problem is that he is too clever for his own good," Francoise had consoled her back at the horse truck that day. "He knows all the dressage moves, but he is easily bored and some days he simply cannot be bothered! That is the price you pay for his genius. When he is bad he is horrid, but when he is in a good mood – he is unbeatable."

Today had definitely been a 'good mood' day. It had

been a fabulous test and as Issie rode back towards the stables Stella came running up to greet her.

"They've posted your scores already!" she said.

"How did we do?" Issie asked as she vaulted down off Nightstorm's back, passing Stella the reins.

"Guess!" Stella said brightly.

"Stella!"

"Come on!" The bubbly redhead grinned. "Take a guess."

"Stella!" Issie took off her top hat and wiped her forehead. "I'm hot, I'm exhausted and I'm not in the mood for guessing games! What was my score?"

Stella pulled a face. "You know you were more fun before you turned pro…"

Issie shot her a glare and Stella laughed. "OK, no messing around. You really want to know? You got thirty-eight!"

Issie's jaw dropped open. In eventing a low score was a good thing. She had been hoping for perhaps something in the forties. But thirty-eight? It was beyond her wildest dreams.

"So where does that put me?" she asked Stella. "Have I made the top ten?"

Stella smiled widely at her best friend. "Better than top ten," she said. "Issie, you're sitting at number three!"

Issie couldn't believe it. A few minutes ago she'd been on the ground dusting the arena sand off her top hat, and now she was on the leaderboard in third place with the cross-country and showjumping, Storm's two best phases, still to come!

As they walked back to the stables, Issie tried to contain her excitement. After all, this was Badminton, the biggest four-star competition in the world, and there was so much that could still go wrong in this dangerous game.

She had no idea how right she was.

CHAPTER 2

With the dressage behind them, the Laurels team were now completely focused on the next phase. The cross-country tomorrow would be the biggest challenge that Issie had ever ridden. Not just because of the size of the fences – although at the maximum height of a metre-twenty they were massive. More than the sheer scale, it was the devilish complexity of the obstacles at Badminton that threatened to trip up even the most experienced equestrians. With demanding combinations of ditches, banks and angled corners, the course was treacherous. It was so tough that half the competitors would fail to finish – many would be eliminated for falls or refusals, while others would retire halfway around when their horses couldn't cope.

While the horses weren't allowed to see the course beforehand, the riders were encouraged to walk around it as many times as they liked.

So far, Issie had walked it three times – and considering the course was a little over six kilometres long, she figured that was a pretty good effort. When Avery suggested they walk it a fourth time after the dressage test, she thought he must be kidding.

"I think we need to take another look at the Vicarage Ditch," Avery said. "I'm still not certain we've got the best path resolved into the spread. It's going to be very hard riding to get your angle right into the jump…"

"Tom," Issie shook her head. "We could walk the course a hundred times but it's not going to make those jumps any smaller. We've figured out my line for that spread. It's going to be fine."

"All the same," Avery said. "I think we should walk the course one last time."

Tom Avery had been Issie's instructor since she first started riding at the Chevalier Point Pony Club. She knew better than to argue with him. And so, she dragged herself up off the sofa in the horse truck and pulled on her boots.

"Let's go then."

The cross-country course began in the main stadium with the flower bed. From there a broad blanket of grassy track led on to the brush, the quarry and then the Huntsman's Close complex which involved a tricky combination and a very acute angle on a corner fence. The lake complex and a broad wooden tabletop fence came after that, and then the trickier narrow obstacles that required precision riding – two round tops and the intricate farmyard fences. After that, the horse had room to gallop until they reached one of the biggest fences on the course. The Vicarage Ditch was a massive obstacle. The ditch itself was almost three metres wide, with a hedge and solid wood rail set into the middle of it, placed at an odd angle.

"So how are you going to face him up to this? Will you turn straight towards the rail?" Avery asked as they walked towards the jump.

Issie frowned. Avery knew exactly how she planned to attack this fence. They had talked it over three times already!

"I'm going to ignore the ditch and take a straight line

at the rail," she said tersely. "It's a big jump so I'll really put my legs on to get a strong canter into it, but Storm and Victory are both fit and they should have loads of energy…"

"…Maybe too much energy," Avery cut her off. "The last thing you want to do is rush it at a gallop and risk mis-timing and crashing into the rail…"

"Well, obviously!" Issie said. "I…"

But Avery had turned his back on her and was now walking the perimeter of the ditch. "I've decided that the best thing to do is to avoid the Vicarage Ditch entirely. If you take the long route here you don't have to jump it, you can go around and take the two offset hedges instead…"

Issie couldn't believe what she was hearing!

"Tom, that's the alternative route! If I avoid the Ditch it will take me three times as long!"

"I know that," Avery said, "but it's the safer option."

"Not if I want to win!" Issie replied. "The long option will add at least ten seconds and that would kill my chances of coming in under the allowed time. I'll be penalised."

"A few time penalties is better than twenty faults from a refusal," Avery argued.

"A few time penalties is all it will take to lose me the competition!"

Issie was stunned that her trainer was suggesting this change at the eleventh hour.

"You've never suggested that I take the soft route before. It's always 'go straight through!' So why the sudden change? Why are you acting so weird?"

"I told you." Avery looked distressed. "It's better to risk the time faults."

"No," Issie shook her head. "It's not…"

"Yes, it jolly well is!" Avery snapped. "It's better to risk the time faults than your horse's life!"

The words hung there in the silence between them. Issie now understood why they were out here standing on the cross-country course, with her instructor in a complete meltdown. This wasn't about her. It wasn't even about Victory and Nightstorm. This was about Avery and something that had happened long ago. She'd been a fool to forget what this jump in particular meant to him. Back in the days when Avery was competing, the Vicarage Ditch was known as the Vicarage Vee. It was this fence that had ended her trainer's professional eventing career. He had fallen here on his horse, The Soothsayer. Avery had come away with minor cuts and bruises, but The Soothsayer had not been so lucky. The horse's life had ended when he broke his leg attempting this fence.

Avery had never spoken to Issie about the accident – in fact he never spoke to anyone about what happened that day. It must have been so painful for Avery to be here now, reliving the agony of that moment all those years ago when he lost his beloved horse.

"I'm so sorry," Issie stammered. "I wasn't thinking…"

Avery's voice was choked with emotion. "I just don't want you to make the same mistake I made," he said.

"I get that, I really do," Issie said gently. "But you're trying to change history. Even if I take the safe route on Victory and Storm, it isn't going to bring *him* back."

She looked her trainer in the eyes. "The alternative route is too slow and I will lose if I take it. You have to let me take the risk and jump the Vicarage Ditch."

Avery sighed, admitting defeat, "When exactly did

you become the smart one in our relationship?"

Issie smiled. "Oh, please! If I'm the smart one then we really are in trouble!"

Avery put his arm around her shoulder. "Come on," he said, "let's go back to the truck. I think you know exactly what you're doing. Straight through the big jumps all the way to home."

They kept the conversation purely on practical matters as they walked back to the truck. This wasn't difficult since there was still so much to prepare for tomorrow. Francoise was running a last-minute check on their tack and equipment. And Stella was down at the stables with both the horses, bedding them in for the evening.

Victory and Storm had both been allocated stalls in the main Badminton House stable block, a stately stone building constructed around a quadrangle courtyard. The main stables took 45 horses, almost half the contingent who were competing over the period of the three-day event, and the loose boxes were beautiful with high ceilings and elegant flagstone floors. They were also high maintenance and Stella had spent most of the day down there, mucking out and replacing Victory and Storm's bedding, organising their feeds and water troughs.

She arrived back at the horse truck at the same time as Issie and Tom, her curly red hair scraped back beneath a cheesecutter cap, which looked like it had been stolen out of Avery's closet. Her jodhpurs were covered in straw and muck, which she made a half-hearted attempt to brush off before she stepped inside the kitchen of the horse truck and collapsed on one of the bench seats.

"Ohmygod!" Stella groaned. "I am exhausted and starving. When is dinner?"

"Dinner," Avery told her, "will be on the table shortly." Stella looked pleased until he added, "…just as soon as you cook it."

In the end, all four of them pitched in to make spaghetti with tomato and tuna sauce and a green salad on the side.

"Carbo loading for tomorrow," Stella told Issie as she dished up a second helping of pasta onto her plate.

"I don't need to fuel up," Issie insisted. "Victory and Storm are the ones who'll be doing the hard work!"

"They've already had their dinner," Stella said. "I

gave them their feeds before I left the stables. Victory bolted his down as usual, but Storm wasn't really that hungry."

There was something about this comment that rang alarm bells for Issie. Storm was a greedy sort, known for snuffling his feed down in five minutes flat and nickering for seconds.

"Was he OK?" Issie asked Stella.

"He was a bit tense," Stella admitted. "You know, after the dressage test, and being somewhere new. He was walking around his stall when I left him, taking little bites of his feed and then wandering away again."

Issie looked up from her plate. "Maybe I should go check on him?"

Avery shook his head. "Issie, you're worrying unnecessarily. Storm is fine, finish your dinner."

It had been the strangest day. Never in her wildest dreams had Issie expected to be in such a strong position after the dressage phase. Her test on Victory had also put her right up there in contention, sitting in eighth place on a score of 39.5.

The real test of courage and ability would come tomorrow. She had put on a brave face in front of Tom and argued that she had to take the Vicarage Ditch head-on. But underneath her bravado, she was worried about her horses too.

She had never lost a horse on the cross-country course, but that didn't mean she didn't understand Avery's pain. She had suffered the same heartbreak – many years ago now – when she had the accident with Mystic.

It had been the day of the Chevalier Point Pony Club Gymkhana, Issie's first-ever competition. Mystic, her beloved pony, had been a total star all day long. The little swaybacked dapple-grey was getting on in years, but he was still a keen jumper and they had just taken out a ribbon in the showjumping class when it happened.

Chevalier Point's resident brat, Natasha Tucker, furious that she'd failed to take first place, had thrown a tantrum and used her whip to take a swipe at her poor pony, Goldrush.

Issie had looked on in horror as the terrified Goldrush

backed away from Natasha to escape and barged into Stella's horse Coco and Kate's gelding Toby, who were tied to a nearby horse truck. The next thing Issie knew, the ponies had pulled loose in fright and bolted, along with Goldrush, heading for the pony-club gates.

As people began to run after the horses, trying to divert them before they reached the main road, Issie realised they'd never catch them in time on foot. But maybe she could stop them on Mystic.

By the time she caught up the ponies were on the main road. Issie had taken one look at the cars whizzing past and then made the fateful decision to follow them. Every moment that the ponies were on that road their lives were in danger, but if she could ride around and herd them back, she might be able to drive them on to the gravel road back to the pony-club grounds.

Her plan worked. She had managed to get the ponies to safety and she was just about to get off the road too when she heard the deep low boom of the truck horn.

As Mystic turned to confront the truck, rising up on his hindquarters, he threw Issie off his back. The last thing she remembered was the sickening screech of the truck tyres and the horrific sound of her pony's terrified whinny. Then her helmet hit the tarmac and everything went black.

In the hospital she woke up with her mother beside her bed, and it was only then that she discovered what had happened. The grey gelding had thrown her clear but it had cost him his life. Mystic was dead.

In the weeks that followed Issie became consumed by grief. Her loss overwhelmed her and she never thought she would be capable of loving another pony ever again.

And then Avery had brought her Blaze. He was working for Horse Welfare and the chestnut mare was a rescue pony that had been placed in his care. When Issie caught sight of the emaciated, terrified mare at the River Paddock she didn't have the heart to turn her away.

Slowly, the broken-spirited mare and the broken-hearted girl began to heal each other and Issie fell in love with Blaze. But she never forgot Mystic. In her heart, she never let him go and the bond between her and the grey pony proved to be more special than Issie had ever imagined.

When Mystic first turned up to help her – alive and real, a flesh-and-blood pony and not some ghostly apparition – Issie should have been astonished, but instead she accepted his presence straight away. She had wished so hard for him to still be there with her, that when he actually came back she never questioned it. They were meant to be together.

In the years that followed, whenever Issie or her horses were in trouble, Mystic would come to her. He was her guardian, her protector and her secret.

While the horses had luxury accommodation at Badminton, Issie and her team weren't quite so well off. Their horse truck was comfortable enough to live in for a few days, but it was a little cramped with four people in it. Avery and his wife Francoise had the double bed in the cavity above the driver's cab, Stella had created a makeshift bed on the banquette seat next to the kitchen table, and Issie was out at the back in the part of the horse truck where the horses themselves usually travelled, on a camping cot bed. It wasn't exactly the

Plaza Hotel, but it suited Issie just fine. She loved the sweet smell of horses and the quiet chirp of crickets right outside as she lay there, trying to get to sleep.

With the cross-country starting at seven-thirty in the morning, an early night was crucial. As Issie had two horses to compete, the organisers had split up her two rides at either end of the day. Her early start was on Storm. The big bay was due in the ten-minute box a little before eight a.m. Victory was her second ride, with a late allocated start time of one-thirty p.m.

Although Nightstorm wasn't due in the box until nearly eight, their day would start much earlier. Stella would be up and grooming him before sunrise and Issie would be down at the stables not long after that. After the exhausting day she'd just had, Issie desperately needed a good night's sleep. Of course, just when you need it most, that's when sleep refuses to do the business. For almost an hour she lay in her cot bed, thinking about the day's events. She was finally beginning to relax, could feel drowsiness overwhelming her, when she heard hoofbeats.

Convinced that the sounds were nothing more than echoes from the stables on the other side of the competitors' park, she ignored them and tried once more to sleep. But in a moment of clarity she sat up, suddenly wide awake. The hoofbeats were too close. They couldn't be coming from the stables.

And then she heard another sound, quite distinct. It was the soft nicker of a horse and it was right outside!

Padding over to the back of the truck in pyjamas and bare feet, Issie pushed open the canvas flap at the rear by the ramp and peered out. It was dark, but there were a few lights on in the competitors' park, providing enough illumination for her to see. There was a horse standing just a few metres away.

Eventing horses tended to be solidly built and at least sixteen hands high. By comparison, the swaybacked grey pony in front of her was tiny, no more than fourteen hands. He stared at her with coal-black eyes, standing so still that he looked like a marble statue. Then he shook his long mane and the statue was suddenly alive and impatient. The gelding gave a snort as if to say, 'Come on! What's keeping you? Let's go already!' Issie couldn't believe it.

It was Mystic.

CHAPTER 3

Mystic stamped a hoof impatiently against the gravel and looked up at Issie, his dark eyes making his intent quite clear. They needed to leave now.

"OK, wait!" Issie ducked back inside the canvas flap and hunted frantically for a pair of boots. Her heart was racing and she couldn't think straight – the fact that Mystic was here now meant that one or both of her horses must be in real trouble. She began to panic. They needed to go now!

There was a sound of hooves and Issie looked back to see Mystic pushing his muzzle through the canvas flap to look for her. She could see his nostrils flare as he sniffed for her. "I'm coming!" she insisted. She unearthed the boots from beneath a pile of coats and pulled them on and pushed her way back out through the canvas flap. Mystic was standing close to the ramp so that Issie could use it as a mounting block. She vaulted on expertly, not worrying that the pony had no saddle or bridle. She had always ridden Mystic like this. She remembered the very first time when they had taken a midnight ride to the pony club from her house. It had been terrifying at first, trying to bounce along bareback at the trot without anything to cling to. But Issie was a far more accomplished rider now. Her natural balance was so honed she relied on her seat alone. Not that it was far to fall anyway if she had come off. Compared to being on big, sixteen-two hand horses like Nightstorm and Victory, the grey pony felt very low to the ground. It had been a long time since Issie last rode Mystic and she was suddenly aware of how much she had grown. She was far too big for him – but Mystic didn't seem to mind. As soon as he felt her weight settled on his back he set off at a brisk trot, weaving between the horse trucks. Issie wrapped her hands in the pony's coarse mane as Mystic trotted his way through the twisting maze of vehicles, heading towards the Badminton House stable block.

It usually took about ten minutes to walk from her truck to the stables, but in a matter of a few minutes the grey pony was pulling up to a halt in the shadows outside the stately stone buildings.

"Good boy!" Issie gave him a slappy pat on the neck and then slid silently to the ground. The grey pony knew he could only take her this far. There was a watchman at night on the gates so she'd need to go alone from this point.

As she ran towards the stable block, Issie cast a glance back over her shoulder at Mystic. She had hoped to catch one last glimpse of his snowy face in the darkness but she should have known better by now. The grey pony was already gone.

As she ran through the entrance gates the security guard dropped the magazine he'd been reading and shone his torch on her.

"Hey, where do you think you're going?" He put out an arm to stop her as she tried to race past.

"I need to get to my horses," Issie said. She was trying to stay calm, but it wasn't easy. Her mind was flashing back to that night in Chevalier Point all those years ago when Storm was stolen. He had been just a colt at the time and the ordeal had been terrifying. Now, Issie was worried that it was happening once more. Had someone come to take her horse? She couldn't stand to go through it again.

"ID tag?" the guard said.

Issie lost her cool. "I'm wearing pyjamas! Does it look like I have my tags on me?"

The guard looked closely at her. "So what's the big hurry about?"

"I need to get to my horses."

The guard looked unimpressed by this vague explanation. "I'm sorry but without tags… hey!"

Before he could say anything more, Issie had ducked under his outstretched arm and was running through the courtyard towards the stable block.

She entered the corridor of the stable block and ran down the row of stalls. Victory was there! She could see him through the bars on the top of the door to his stall. He seemed to be totally fine.

"Hey, you!" Issie could hear the guard running up the corridor behind her but she ignored him and continued on to the next stall.

"Storm?"

Her breath was coming in gasps as her throat constricted with nerves. Her heart was racing. When she reached the door to his loose box she half-expected to find his stall empty, her best horse taken from her once again. But Storm was still there too!

Relieved to see him, Issie collapsed against the loose box door and put her face up to the bars.

"Hey, boy!" Issie smiled at him. "I'm glad you're OK. I was worried about…"

The smile disappeared from her face. Storm usually came to the door to greet her, but he was acting like he wasn't even aware that Issie was there. He seemed preoccupied. He kept turning his head around to look at his flank and then lifting his hind leg to kick at his belly.

Issie was confused. She had seen Blaze behave like this once when the mare was about to have a foal. But Storm was a stallion. He wasn't about to give birth, so why was he behaving like…

Suddenly, the big bay dropped to his knees in the loose box and began to roll. At that moment, Issie knew what was wrong. She was about to slide the bolt to his stall when she felt a hand clasp her roughly on the arm.

"You're in serious trouble!"

It was the security guard. His face was flushed from sprinting and he was clearly furious.

"No!" Issie turned to him, "You don't understand. I've got to get in there! Look at him!"

Storm was lying down on the straw bedding of his stall, and rolling frantically from side to side, grunting in pain.

"He's got colic!" Issie said. "If we let him roll he'll end up killing himself! He'll twist his bowel and then he'll die!"

The guard let go of her arm. He was an officious sort, but he had also been hired because he was a skilled horseman and he knew immediately that Issie's assessment of the bay stallion was probably right. Colic was like a very painful stomach ache – and the horse would keep rolling to try and relieve the pain. But the rolling would actually make matters much worse. The situation could very quickly turn deadly if they didn't act fast.

"Let's get him up!" the guard said, reaching out to pull back the sliding doors of the box.

Issie was already way ahead of him. She reached for the halter and lead rope that were hanging by the stall door and slipped the halter over Storm's head. The stallion was still lying down and even as Issie tried to buckle the halter up, he was attempting to roll again.

"Hey, no, Storm," Issie said, trying her best to subdue her own panic and speak gently to the horse. "Easy, boy, don't roll. I'm here now. We're going to get you up on your feet…"

But Storm wasn't listening. As Issie tried to secure the buckle on the halter he flung his head up, narrowly missing her face. She reeled backwards and before she could grasp the halter again Storm had flung himself to the ground, legs flailing over his head. Issie was forced to flatten herself against the stable wall to avoid the flying hooves.

"Storm! Stop it!" There was a wild look in the stallion's eyes. He was in so much pain that he wasn't listening at all. A wall had gone up between them and she couldn't get through.

Issie looked at her beautiful horse, writhing in agony. She had to pull herself together and act now if she wanted to save him.

Avoiding the thrashing hooves, Issie stepped closer to Storm's head and shouted out to the security guard.

"I'm going to need your help! Can you get to the side of him and prepare to push?"

The guard immediately grasped her plan and backed his way around the loose box, avoiding Storm's legs which were still waving violently in the air, until he'd managed to get himself into position near the stallion's flank.

"Stay back from him until I tell you to move!" Issie told him.

The guard nodded. He wasn't arguing. Those hooves were deadly weapons.

Storm stopped thrashing for a moment, and Issie immediately seized the chance and lunged forward to grab the lead rope. "Do it now!" she yelled at the guard. With an almighty heave, she gave a yank on the rope while the guard put his shoulder to the stallion's side and shoved against the horse as hard as he could.

With a grunt of effort, the stallion heaved himself up to his feet, and immediately repaid the guard's efforts by lashing out at him with a hind leg.

"Are you OK?" Issie asked.

The guard nodded. "He missed me."

"I'm so sorry," Issie said. "He's just in so much pain…"

The guard looked pale with shock. "Well, let's get him outside into the courtyard. You need to keep him moving."

Issie had never looked after a horse with colic before, but like most riders she knew the drill. Keep them walking, keep them calm and, no matter what, don't let them roll.

But keeping Storm moving wasn't an easy matter. The stallion was in terrible pain and all he wanted to do was lie down again. He tried once more to drop to his knees and Issie had to bellow at him and yank sharply on the lead rope to make him step forward and leave the stall.

Even when they were out in the stony courtyard, Storm was still reluctant to walk. It was taking all of Issie's strength and patience just to keep him moving.

"Will you be OK while I go and call the vet?" the guard asked her, looking worried.

Issie nodded. "It's OK, I can handle him. Go make the call."

The guard must have only been gone for ten minutes but it felt like a lifetime as Issie walked Storm around the yard alone. She could feel her own stomach tying in knots. Her horse had colic, but everything depended on what happened next. If she could stop Storm from injuring himself further, and if the vet arrived in time, then the stallion still had a chance of survival.

She thought back to Stella's comment that the stallion had been off his feed. Why hadn't she followed through and come down to the stables to check on him? Had Storm been in this state for long or had the colic set in quickly? Issie put out a hand to reassure the horse and realised that his whole body was drenched with sweat.

"It's going to be OK, boy, they'll be back soon..." she reassured the stallion. But inside she was panicking. *Where was the guard? He'd been gone for far too long!*

Suddenly there were voices in the darkness. The guard was back – and he had the vet with him.

"I'm Maurice Cross," the vet introduced himself with a brisk handshake. He dropped his medical case to the ground, dug out a stethoscope and began to examine Storm straight away.

"So he's showing signs of colic?"

"He's been getting to the ground and trying to roll,"

Issie confirmed. She ran through the rest of Storm's symptoms while the vet examined his heart rate and breathing.

"His pulse is very high," the vet looked concerned. "He's at over 100 beats per minute at the moment."

"Is that bad?" Issie asked. "Is he going to be OK?"

The vet shook his head. "I can't tell you that yet. There are different types of colic. If it's just a nervous muscle spasm then he'll recover overnight. But if it's something more serious, like a twist in his bowel or an impaction, then he'll deteriorate in the next few hours…"

The vet stopped talking and began to hunt about in his bag. He pulled out a hypodermic needle and loaded the syringe with clear fluid.

"We'll give him a muscle relaxant and see what happens," the vet said. "With any luck, he's having spasmodic contractions and the relaxant will help to ease them."

The vet took the hypodermic needle and thrust it firmly into the muscle of Storm's neck. The stallion didn't flinch as the needle went in all the way to the hilt.

"It should take effect in a few minutes," the vet said. "The main thing now is to keep walking him. It's vital that you don't let him roll."

The vet gestured towards the security gates at the front of the yard. "They have my number on speed dial," he told her. "I'll come back and check on you in the morning. But don't be afraid to call me before then if there's any change."

Issie watched the vet leave and hoped that a phone call wouldn't be necessary.

"Is there anything I can do?" The night guard was clearly feeling awful that he had tried to turf her out earlier. "Do you want me to lead him for you for a while?"

Issie shook her head. She couldn't bring herself to leave Storm's side, not even for a moment.

"Can you do me a favour?" she asked. "I need you to make a phone call for me."

By the time Avery, Francoise and Stella arrived at the yard the vet's injection had begun to work and

Storm's pains seemed to be easing, but the stallion was still distressed and Issie still needed to keep him moving.

"It looks like we might be lucky," Francoise said gently to Issie. "If the pains are lessening then the chances are that he has spasmodic colic. It is painful – but it is the best kind of colic to get – he'll get better again quite quickly."

"It's not because I overfed him, is it?" Stella looked distraught. "I gave him a regular feed…"

Francoise shook her head. "No – this kind of colic attack is usually brought on by nerves and stress, not food. He needs to be walked for the rest of the night, but the chances are good that he will recover."

Avery agreed. "It looks like the muscle relaxant is working."

"Will I be able to ride him tomorrow?" Issie asked. "It's only a few hours until the cross-country."

Avery shook his head. "It's too soon. Even if all of his symptoms were gone by then, riding him would be a huge risk. He could develop a second bout and it would kill him."

Issie's heart plummeted. If you had asked her an hour

ago she would have wept with gratitude just knowing that her horse was going to live – but to have her dreams yanked away like this… ohmygod, they were in the top three after the dressage! It was too cruel. But she knew what she had to do.

She couldn't ride – she had to retire. She was pulling Storm out of Badminton.

CHAPTER 4

Issie felt like she had only just fallen asleep when she was being woken up by the glare of bright sunlight on her face. The canvas flap of the truck had been opened up and it was daylight outside.

"Oops!" Stella quickly shut the canvas behind her again. "Sorry! Didn't mean to wake you!" She reached across Issie and began rummaging around in a gear bag until she found a roll of gamgee bandage.

Issie sat up, still feeling groggy. "What time is it?"

"It's nearly ten," Stella said.

Ten! No wonder the sky had looked so blue. She should have been awake hours ago. The cross-country would be underway already!

"It's OK. Everything is under control," Stella said. "Tom told me to leave you to sleep in."

Nightstorm's bout of colic had kept Issie up until the early hours of the morning. She hadn't wanted to leave her horse's side but at five a.m. Avery finally insisted that she go back and get some sleep.

"Stella will stay with him," Avery told her. "You need to rest. You've still got Victory to ride tomorrow."

Stella finished packing the gamgee bandages in the kit bag and slung it over her shoulder.

"Storm's doing much better," she said, anticipating Issie's question. "Maurice came to check on him again at around eight this morning and he's pretty sure that he's over the worst of it. He might have a few more stomach pains over the next twenty-four hours but he's going to make a complete recovery."

"Thanks, Stella," Issie said gratefully.

Stella looked like she was going to burst into tears. "I'm so sorry, Issie. I should have realised when he wasn't eating that something was wrong..."

"There was no way you could have known he was going to get colic," Issie told her.

Stella looked miserable. "You should be riding him

today. He would have gone clear around that cross-country course. I know it."

Issie swallowed down hard on her disappointment. She didn't want to make Stella feel any worse, but deep down she was devastated. Yesterday she had been in third place after the dressage. Now, her hopes of taking the trophy on the big bay stallion were destroyed. But her chances weren't completely lost. She still had her second mount to ride. She had to pull herself together, get out of bed and get ready for battle. Victory was due to tackle the four-star course that afternoon.

The green fields of Badminton Estate, usually populated by sheep, were home to over a hundred and fifty thousand spectators on cross-country day. Everywhere that Issie looked there were people crammed up against the rope barriers, all trying to get into the best possible position to see the action.

The Tannoy crackled, then Mike Partridge resumed his commentary. "What a morning it has been! The course here at Badminton has proved to be one of the most challenging in the history of the event and has upset many a combination of horse and rider. Only five clear rounds have been completed so far. Gerhardt Muller on Velluto Rosso is hoping to add to that tally and make it six. He's clear so far as they head towards the water complex…"

As Issie rode Victory into the warm-up arena, she caught sight of William Fox-Pitt and Piggy French, both mounted up and ready to ride and her heart skipped a beat. The most famous faces in the sport of eventing were here today and the atmosphere in the stadium was electric.

Issie still couldn't quite believe that she was about to ride one of the most famous cross-country courses in the world!

Don't think about the pressure, she told herself firmly, *focus on the task ahead.* She looked across the main arena and concentrated her eye on the first fence, the flowerbed. From there, she let her mind ride the course, mentally cantering and galloping through it, committing to memory the turns and checks that she would make before each obstacle. As she did this, she was only slightly aware that Victory too was beginning to grow tense.

The brown gelding was swishing his tail in consternation. Tacked up in his cross-country kit, his front and hind legs smothered with white grease to help him to slide more easily over the solid jumps, he knew that their time had almost come. He was keyed up and anxious to get out on the course and there was already a lather of white sweat on his neck from anticipation as Avery took hold of his reins and led him towards the start box.

"There have been quite a few run-outs at that brush element in Huntsman's Close," Avery told Issie as he walked her forward. "Make sure you keep your line to that corner and don't rush it."

"OK," Issie nodded.

"And kick on as you come into the water. You need to get three big strides in before you strike that middle element. A lot of riders have tried to put in a fourth stride and come to grief."

Even though he had already checked her girth at least five times, Avery now gave it one more final check. Issie noticed that he was trembling a little as he took the girth straps in his hands. Her trainer looked up at her and that was when she saw the concern in his eyes.

Issie knew exactly what he was thinking. The Badminton cross-country course was six and a half kilometres of hard galloping and enormous fences. Considered to be the ultimate test of fitness in a horse, it was also a test of rider stamina – and after last night's drama in the stables Issie was sleep-deprived and running on empty. Tackling a course like this in her condition was dangerous. All it would take was a moment's inattention, a fleeting loss of focus, and she would be in big trouble. This fear was etched over Avery's face. He knew just how challenging this course was and he was desperately worried about her.

"Issie…" Avery began.

She cut him off before he could say anything more. "Tom, please, don't. I'll be fine."

Issie wasn't giving up – not now! Victory was still in with a real chance. They had been in eighth place after the dressage but already over the past few hours the cross-country course had taken its toll on the leaderboard. Eliminations and refusals in the top ranks meant that a clear round on the cross-country would elevate Issie up to fifth place at the very least.

Avery saw the look of grim determination on her face

and he knew he would never be able to change her mind. "Good luck," he said. "Remember, if in doubt..."

"I know," Issie grinned at him, "kick on!"

Avery let go of the reins and Issie had a few final seconds to make her last adjustments, checking her compulsory airtech inflatable vest and setting the stopwatch on her wrist. She had the timer set so that she knew exactly where she needed to be on the clock at the minute markers around the course. It wasn't good enough to go clear – she would have to avoid time penalties too.

Issie tightened her grip on the reins and urged Victory into the box. The gelding tried to leap forward and Issie had to pull hard on the reins, turning a circle in the box behind the start line.

"Easy, boy," Issie said to him in a soft voice, "Any minute now..."

She clasped the reins in one hand and placed the other hand on the stopwatch button as the starting steward spoke into his walkie-talkie to confirm that the other competitors out on the course were far enough ahead.

"We're all clear to jump 12," the voice at the other end of the walkie-talkie crackled. "You can let the next rider go."

Issie felt a tight knot of nerves strangling her stomach. This was it.

"OK, line him up." The steward waited for her to edge Victory forward in the box. "And ready, get set… and go!"

As Victory surged forward across the start line the electronic timer let out a peep. They were off! The crowds in the stands cheered as they came in to take the first fence.

Victory leapt the flowerbed like a seasoned professional, taking the jump with a perfect forward stride. Issie suddenly exhaled and realised that she had been holding her breath until that point. It was always good to get the first jump out of the way. Now she was really doing this. Her nerves were gone and she was totally focused on the ride ahead as they came along the rolling green turf, past the cheering crowd at the grandstand exit, veering to the left to approach jump number two, the massive Higham's Brush. Victory took this fence precisely, and Issie felt her confidence levels surging. She was so elated that she briefly lost focus and they were only a few strides out from the quarry when she realised they were at full gallop and needed to slow down. There was a massive drop on the far side of this fence and they were taking it too fast!

There was no time to pull up. Issie and Victory flew the fence, jumping far too big and landing halfway down the bank on the other side. Issie quickly recovered and shortened the horse up in time for the next fence, a big log positioned at the top of a bank. They took the log by the skin of their teeth.

Wake up! she told herself angrily. She had to prepare for the fences ahead and be ready each time if she wanted to get around this course in one piece.

At the infamous Huntsman's Close, she found herself fretting about the big corner hedge. It was set in the shade of some spreading elm trees and it was easy for horses to be bewildered by the tree shadows and unable to see the hedge until the moment it confronted them.

Preparing Victory for the corner, Issie set him back on his hocks after the first element and collected him up so that he had plenty of time to eye up the hedge and take it very neatly on a lovely forward stride.

"Magnificent! Just look at this horse!" Mike Partridge was enthusing to the crowd. "He is absolutely eating this course up. But how will he handle the lake complex? Remember, Isadora only got given the ride on this wonderful eventer when he deposited his rider, Warren Woodfield, in the drink with a spectacular fall into the water at the Adelaide Three-Day event. Warren ended up with a broken back for his troubles and has been out of competition ever since. So, has this horse lost his nerve when it comes to water?"

Coming into the lake complex, Issie already knew the answer to this question. Since then Issie had jumped several three-star water complexes on the horse. She knew that he'd lost none of his nerve.

At the front of the water jump Issie could see two Mitsubishi flatbed pick-up trucks. They were parked tail-to-tail with their flatbeds touching and there were pretty flower planters sitting on their open platforms. However the flowers didn't in any way camouflage the fact that these were trucks – and they were intended to be jumped!

Squaring up to the massive spread of the pick-up

trucks, Issie put her legs on firmly and kicked on to the jump to make sure that there was no doubt in Victory's mind that they were going over this obstacle. She needn't have worried. Victory knew exactly what to do and he flew the flatbeds and cantered onwards into the water, taking one-two-three canter strides before leaping the narrow element in the middle of the pond. Then he cantered on and over the last jump and out the other side.

"Beautifully handled!" Mike Partridge was impressed. "A lovely round so far for this young rider!"

Through the water and over the broad barn table and then coming down into the country complex, Issie was really hitting her stride. She had checked her watch at the minute marker as she whizzed by at a gallop and was absolutely smack on time.

They were coming down the long, sweeping run of green lawn to the Farmyard, the last jump before the Vicarage Ditch, when suddenly a whistle blew and a steward in a high-vis jacket stepped out onto the course and waved his hands to tell her to stop.

Issie ignored him at first, thinking that there must be some mistake. Why would a steward be stopping her? She'd done nothing wrong. She had walked this course so many times she knew it like the back of her hand and she was certain that she hadn't taken a wrong turn.

As she tried to gallop on, another steward appeared on the course and blew his whistle, waving his hands vigorously. There was no doubt about it. They were stopping her.

It wasn't easy pulling Victory up. The brown gelding had been in full gallop and he knew that there were more jumps to come. He didn't want to stop, and when he did halt at last his flanks were heaving and he was wet with sweat.

"What have I done?" Issie wanted to know.

"It's not you," the steward said. "It's another rider, further ahead. We needed to stop you to give us time to clear the jump so you can continue."

Issie's blood ran cold. She knew the rider directly ahead of her on the course. It was the Austrian competitor Gerhardt Muller, a man who was well known on the circuit and had ridden against Issie just a couple of weeks ago in Kentucky. Today he was on one of his best horses, the much admired liver chestnut mare, Velluto Rosso.

"Is it Gerhardt?" Issie asked the steward. "Is he OK?"

The steward looked uncomfortable, clearly unsure how much he was allowed to say. "He's had an accident at the Vicarage Ditch. The ambulance is with him now. Keep your horse circling and as soon as we can give you the all-clear we'll let you go again and you'll be back on the clock."

The clock! Ohmygod! When the steward had pulled Issie to a stop, that meant the clock had been stopped on Issie's round. But Issie hadn't stopped the watch on her own wrist.

She clicked to pause it now, but it was way too late. She had no idea how many seconds had already ticked by – maybe even a whole minute or more. Now she had no way of keeping track of her time from here around the rest of this course. Even worse, with every minute that ticked by while she waited, Victory was getting cold. They had just been getting into their rhythm but now their momentum had been destroyed. It was the worst possible place to stop because the jumps ahead were the biggest and most demanding on the course. The Farmyard Complex was a series of difficult wooden corners combined with a hay cart. And straight after that was the Vicarage Ditch! She had been hoping to come into that massive spread with a head of steam up after having galloped half the course. Instead, they were walking around in a holding pattern, waiting for the course to clear. The stewards were muttering into their walkie-talkies. She heard one of them say that Gerhardt had been loaded on to the ambulance. She wondered what had happened to him. If the Vicarage Ditch really was jumping badly then maybe she should be taking the long route after all?

The steward spoke once more into his walkie-talkie and then he turned at last to Issie. "They're about to let you back onto the course again. Get ready…"

A few moments later the whistle blew and Issie was galloping once more. In total, she had spent nearly fifteen minutes being held back. She was now on a horse that was cold and tense as she came in to attack the Farmyard.

Victory stood back a little from the first corner and took it clumsily, but he took the second corner much better and he flew over the third element, the hay cart.

Issie felt a rush of adrenalin as they took the cart and she knew that there was no way they were taking the alternate route at the Vicarage Ditch. They were going straight through.

She gave Victory a quick tap with the whip as they galloped down the approach to the fence, just to let him know that something really big was looming ahead. Victory raised his head at the sight of the massive wooden rail set into the middle of a three-metre-wide ditch. His ears pricked forward and his strides shortened up. They were three strides out when Issie kicked on like crazy and asked him to stretch out once more. Victory powered forward for all he was worth and took the Vicarage Ditch beautifully, soaring over it and landing expertly on the other side. Behind the crowd barriers the spectators went wild. Their cheers followed Issie around the rest of the course as she cleared fence after fence including the famous Shogun Hollow, the Staircase, the Owl Hole and the Rolex Crossing. As they came in to take the final fence in the main arena, the Mitsubishi Garden, the audience were on their feet and hollering their support.

"Flying in over that last fence!" Mike Partridge said.

"She's come in against the odds, but the big question is, has she made it within the time?"

There was no point looking at her watch and so Issie waited like everyone else for the announcer to break the news.

"Ladies and gentlemen," Mike Partridge's voice had a serious tone, "she hasn't come in on time… she's *beaten* the clock by *two whole seconds*! Isadora Brown has romped in – it's a clear round!"

CHAPTER 5

Issie and Avery arrived back at the horse truck that afternoon to find an unexpected guest on their doorstep.

"I know it's a little premature for celebrations," Tulia Disbrowe said, handing Avery a bottle of champagne, "but I thought I would wish you all good luck for tomorrow."

Tulia Disbrowe's flight from Australia had been delayed and she had missed seeing her horse compete in the dressage. However, she made it in time to witness Victory's superb cross-country round.

"That was a remarkable piece of riding," she told Issie. "I honestly thought it was over when I saw you being pulled up by the stewards. It's so hard to bring a horse back on to form after a stop like that. But you got him back on track for the second half, beautifully handled!"

Issie brushed off the compliment. "Your boy is such a star, Tulia. He answered every question and jumped perfectly."

"Best of all," Avery said, "he's come through the course totally sound and ready for the showjumping tomorrow."

Victory had indeed coped better than any of them could have hoped. He had finished the six kilometres with only a few superficial cuts and scrapes – although Avery wasn't taking any chances and had Stella down at the stables now, keeping the horse's legs iced to take down any potential swelling in preparation for tomorrow.

The trotting-up was first thing in the morning. The horses would be led out on the tarmac in front of three judges who had to approve their soundness before the competitors would be allowed to progress on to the showjumping phase.

Stella and Avery both insisted that Victory was in fine

fettle and the trotting up would be little more than a formality. But after Nightstorm's unexpected bout of colic, Issie wasn't taking anything for granted. She stared at the bottle of champagne that Avery had left next to the tack box in the back of the horse truck and couldn't help feeling that they weren't quite ready for celebrations. Not yet.

After much nagging from Stella after the Kentucky Four-Star, Issie had gone out and chosen a new outfit especially for the trotting-up. It was a pale blue dress with a full skirt and Issie had teamed it with a black jacket over the top and a pair of black and cream ballet pumps.

"Too girly?" she asked Stella and Francoise as she paraded in the stables that morning.

"It's gorgeous!" Stella said.

"*Très belle!*" Francoise enthused. "The judges will be so busy looking at you they will never notice whether the horse is lame!"

"That's the plan," Issie said.

Over the years, the ritual of the trotting-up had

become almost as much of a spectator event as the showjumping. That morning hundreds of onlookers gathered on the forecourt of the magnificent Badminton House to watch the riders each take their turn to trot their perfectly groomed horses inhand for the judging panel.

Issie waited with Victory, her stomach tied in knots with nerves. When her turn came, the brown gelding was passed without hesitation. The same could not be said for two of the big names in the competition – Millie Wardlaw and Tim Smith – when their horses were spun.

The shock eliminations at the eleventh hour spelt disaster for Millie and Tim. They had been in second and fourth place respectively and with their exclusion from the showjumping phase Issie and Victory moved up the leaderboard. They were now lying in an incredible third place!

Even more exciting, only three faults were now separating the top three riders – Andrew Pember-Reeves was in the lead on Mythic Realm, still on his dressage score of 37. Prudence Palmer and her horse The Changeling were in second place with time faults that pushed their score to 39. Issie was breathing down her neck on 39.5. There was only one rail separating the top three and suddenly the talk was starting at Badminton about the prospect of Issie Brown edging her way to the winner's podium and keeping her hopes alive for completing the Grand Slam!

The odds were stacked against anyone achieving the three-events-in-a-row victory, but now that she lay in third place, the goal was once again within reach, and the buzz surrounding her chances resurfaced.

"The tension in the air is palpable," Mike Partridge intoned. "This next young competitor has to keep all the rails up if she wants to stay in with a chance of winning Badminton."

As she cantered into the showjumping arena, Issie knew that everything was riding on this round. If she didn't go clear in the arena then her chances were over. The pressure on her now was intense – could she handle it and bring Victory home without a mistake?

A hush fell over the crowd as the bell sounded and Issie circled Victory in a collected canter to come through the flags and confront the first jump – a blue upright.

This was the moment when Victory's calibre as an

eventer would be truly tested. Yesterday the gelding had been fearless and bold, taking the knocks as he bashed his way around six kilometres of solid, rough-hewn jumps. Now, here in the showjumping ring, a totally different mindset was required. Victory needed to pick up his feet carefully over every fence to avoid bumping the delicately balanced rails if they wanted to take home the gold.

Issie felt her heart hammering in her chest as Victory took a sluggish approach to the first jump and dragged his hind legs over the fence. Was the brown gelding more exhausted than any of them had suspected? Would this phase prove to be too much for him?

The pole rocked but it didn't fall and Issie collected the horse up and rode him firmly towards the next jump. If Victory was tired, then it was up to her to help him get round the course.

At the second fence, she rode with precision and determination and Victory seemed to wake up and lift his game, clearing the jump with air to spare. This was more like it!

Issie urged him on towards the double, putting her legs on firmly. Victory responded a little too well. He cleared the first jump but the excess energy in his stride left him off balance for the next fence and he took one long stride and leapt from too far back. His hind legs scraped the pole as he went over the jump and once again the rail rocked in its cups.

Issie wanted so badly to turn around and see if the rail had fallen, but she knew it would be fatal. *Don't look back*, she told herself, *stay focused on the next fence.*

"She's still clear," Mike Partridge confirmed. "The rail hasn't fallen. Now she takes a sharp turn and in to confront the big spread, the red and white rails…"

The red and white spread was a huge jump and Victory was all class as he took off perfectly and cleared it. The brown gelding's neck was white and frothy with sweat and his breath was coming in keen snorts as they turned to take the white gate and then the treble. This time the striding was perfect and they popped in and out with a single stride between each fence and didn't drop a rail.

With just three jumps standing between her and a clear round, Issie was doing her best to keep her cool. But as she came at the oxer she realised she had totally messed up her line, and her canter lead was wrong.

Luckily, Victory was the ultimate schoolmaster. He saw that he was on the wrong leg and did an amazing flying change, righting himself in time and putting in a little short stride right in front of the jump to make it work. Issie held her breath, worried that Victory would bring a hind leg down on the back rail, but nothing fell. She kept her eyes ahead to the next fence. Only two more jumps to go and she would be clear.

At the penultimate jump there was a heart-stopping moment when they took the fence too fast and Issie panicked that Victory wouldn't take off in time – but again his talent showed through and he got his knees up just enough to clear the rails.

All this time they had been belting around the course between the fences, cantering as fast as they dared to try and stay inside the time. And with one jump to go Issie wasn't slowing down. Coming in at a fast canter she rode hard at the jump and relied on her horse to find the perfect take-off point. Victory obliged, arcing beautifully and clearing the final fence with half a metre to spare.

As she crossed the line a roar came up from the crowd.

"It's a clear round, and no time faults!" Mike Partridge confirmed.

Now Issie's fate rested with the other two riders who were yet to come. Prudence Palmer on The Changeling was in the arena next and then the current number one on the leaderboard, Andrew Pember-Reeves on Mythic Realm. A knocked-down rail from both Andrew and Prudence would give Issie the win that she so desperately needed.

Vaulting down off Victory's back, Issie joined her teammates on the sidelines and watched with her stomach doing flip-flops as Prudence Palmer entered the ring. Prudence's mare, The Changeling, was a stunning dapple-grey Thoroughbred that Issie had admired when she first saw the pair compete at the Stars of Pau in France. Today The Changeling looked on perfect form as she swept over one fence after the other without so much as grazing a rail. As she came down through the treble there was a moment of tension as the mare scraped hard against the rail of the second element, but the fence still didn't fall. With only three fences to go before Prudence completed a clear round, Issie's heart was in her mouth and Stella was gripping onto her arm so hard that Issie thought she would cut off the circulation!

Please! Oh please! It was awful, wishing that a rail would fall, but that was exactly what Issie found herself doing.

But nothing fell at the treble or the oxer. The Changeling was over the upright now and the mare was still clear with only one fence left to go. As Prudence lined the grey horse up and rode at the jump Issie watched in dismay as the mare flew the fence and galloped on through the flags.

Prudence Palmer and The Changeling had just dashed Issie's chances of the Grand Slam with a clear round!

As the crowd cheered and went wild for Prudence, Issie clapped too. It had been a good round and even though it meant bitter disappointment for her, she had to give Prudence credit for riding so well.

The shock came a moment later when Mike Partridge's voice was surprisingly somber over the loudspeakers.

"A clear round for Prudence Palmer but I'm afraid she has gone over the time limit by three seconds and has earnt herself one and a half penalties. This pushes her back into third place."

Issie was numb with shock. There had only been half a penalty between her and Prudence and the time faults were enough to tip the balance! The Changeling had slipped down the leaderboard and Issie and Victory had risen up to second place!

"It will take more than time faults to knock Andrew Pember-Reeves from his top spot," Mike Partridge clarified as the last rider of the day entered the ring.

"Andrew has a two and a half point lead over Isadora Brown and there is no way that time penalties will get the better of him. It will take a rail down to cost him the Badminton Horse Trials."

On the sidelines, Issie's team had gathered around her. Stella had completely forgotten that she was supposed to be untacking Victory and cooling him down. She was standing beside Issie, transfixed by the action in the main arena. On the other side of Issie, Avery had taken off his cheesecutter cap and was raking a hand anxiously through his curly brown hair until finally Francoise stopped him by grasping his hand in her own for reassurance.

Andrew's horse, Mythic Realm, was a handsome dark brown warmblood with a thick white blaze and two hind socks. Issie watched as Andrew set the gelding up for the first jump and then felt her heart palpitate as Mythic Realm knocked the top rail on the first fence and it shook hard in its cups.

"Ohmygod!" Stella put her hands over her eyes. "I can't watch. I can't watch…"

Issie wanted it all to be over, but for some reason time seemed to go into slow motion and every single fence seemed to take an eternity.

At fence after fence, Mythic Realm continued to jump clear. The gelding was taking the rails in superb style and as he neatly cleared the treble, Issie felt her heart sink. Only three jumps to go and Andrew Pember-Reeves looked totally in control.

"This is looking very good indeed," Mike Partridge breathed over the loudspeaker, "all clear at the third to last fence – only two more now to go…"

Issie could feel the trophy slipping away. She told herself that it didn't matter. Second place at Badminton was still better than her wildest dreams and…

The clatter of falling rails shattered her thoughts. Mythic Realm had just smashed through the top two rails of the second to last fence!

In the stands the crowd gasped in horror. Then, just moments later, there were cries of utter disbelief as Mythic Realm bounded on to take the next fence down too! Andrew Pember-Reeves looked devastated as he rode out of the arena. He had racked up eight faults and slipped right down the leaderboard all the way to fifth place.

On the loudspeaker Mike Partridge summed up the situation. "Tragedy in the final moments for Andrew Pember-Reeves – and history in the making for young Isadora Brown! The seventeen-year-old from Chevalier Point takes home the winner's laurels here at Badminton and *that* means she remains on track in her bid for the greatest prize of all – the Grand Slam!"

"Issie!" Stella was still gripping her arm so hard that Issie was worried she might cut off the circulation. "Issie! You've won it! You have to go back in there and do your victory lap!"

Issie looked dumbfounded. "Tom?"

Avery was wide-eyed. He tried to speak and was at a loss for words for a moment. Then he pulled himself together. "Come on," he said, "I'll give you a leg up. You need to get in there!"

As they did their lap of the grandstand, Issie was

certain that Victory knew the applause was for him. Showing off for the crowds, the brown gelding put on a burst of speed, galloping down the side of the arena, and Issie felt the hairs on the back of her neck standing up on end. It was the most incredible sensation – to be taking the winner's lap at the Badminton Horse Trials!

The prize-giving that followed was a grand ceremony as the Duke of Beaufort handed her the silver trophy featuring the three iconic horses, representing the three phases of eventing. The trophy was so heavy that when the photographer asked Issie to hold it aloft for a picture she struggled to lift it.

As was customary, Victory's owner, Tulia Disbrowe, was in the winner's circle with them for the presentation. Issie had expected Tulia to accompany them back to the stables afterwards, but after congratulating Issie on her win Tulia had oddly excused herself the minute they left the arena.

Victory was fed and watered and the team all gathered back at the horse truck – except for Tulia who was nowhere to be found and wasn't answering her phone. "Where the blazes has she got to?" Avery said, trying her mobile yet again. "She should be here! That champagne needs to be opened..."

As he said this, there was a knock at the door and a moment later Tulia Disbrowe entered.

"Tulia!" Avery opened his arms to welcome her in. "Excellent! We can start the party at last!"

There was the pop of a cork and glasses were filled.

"Congratulations, Issie!" Francoise said, raising her glass up in celebration. "Two in a row! Now you only have Burghley to go!"

Stella was grinning from ear to ear. "I think I'm still in shock! That was the most brilliant clear round!"

"Tulia?" Avery said. "Would you like to say a few words?"

"Actually," Tulia stepped forward. "I do have something to say."

She turned to Issie. "I want you to know that you did a fantastic job out there today – in fact, over the past three days. I couldn't have wished for a better jockey for Victory – which is what makes this so difficult..."

"What are you talking about?" Issie said.

"I've just spent the past hour in negotiations with a very influential horse syndicate," Tulia said. "They approached me today and offered me an absolutely exorbitant amount of money. In the end I couldn't say no."

"Money? For what?"

"For Victory," Tulia Disbrowe said. "I've sold the horse."

Ever since last night, Issie had been fighting this feeling of dread, like a sixth sense that something was wrong. Now she realised her intuition had been right all along.

"So, what does that mean for me?" Issie asked. "Do I still have the ride?"

Tulia put down her champagne glass. "The syndicate want to put their own jockey on him. They're taking over his training – effective immediately."

Issie had won the Badminton Horse Trials, but in a cruel twist of fate she was now being separated from the horse that had made it all possible. She had lost Victory.

CHAPTER 6

There was a stunned silence in the horse truck and then Avery exploded in anger. "Are you telling me that this syndicate want to get rid of the rider who just won the Badminton Horse Trials? Are they mad?"

Tulia looked taken aback. "Tom, I can understand how upset you are. I was surprised by this decision too. But the syndicate has bought the horse and they have the right to choose their own rider."

"So that's it, is it?" Avery fumed. "They offered you the money and you took it, regardless of the consequences? Without a second thought for Issie…"

Tulia's demeanour suddenly turned icy. "Tom, you know as well as I do that in business it's always about money. Look at Edward Gal. He had broken every world record riding Totilas, but they still sold the horse out from under him. These things happen at the top of the game. I'm sorry, but that's the way it is!"

Avery glared at Tulia. "And you didn't even think to discuss it with us before you took the cheque?"

"I didn't have to," Tulia replied bluntly. "The horse belongs to me and I have every right to make the decision to sell. Tom, no one is taking anything away from Isadora's achievements, but at the end of the day I had to think about the future and what is best for Victory."

"You must be joking!" Avery's fury reached new heights. "How dare you act as if…"

"Tom!" Issie shook her head. "Can't you see it's no use? It won't change anything."

Issie stepped up to Tulia Disbrowe. "How long before they come for him?"

"It's all been organised. The head of the syndicate is collecting him within the hour," Tulia said.

Issie didn't say anything more – she walked straight past Tulia and headed for the door.

"Issie?" Tulia said. "Where are you going?"

Issie looked back at her, her eyes filled with tears, "Where do you think, Tulia? I'm going to see Victory. I'm saying goodbye!"

As she walked to the stables, Issie was overwhelmed by anger and disbelief. It was so brutally unfair! She had spent the past year working on her relationship with Victory so that the horse trusted her completely and would do anything for her. She had raised him to the very top and this was the thanks she got! The syndicate hadn't even had the decency to give her one day of happiness to enjoy her win before they stole the horse away from her.

The stables were busy with riders packing down and mucking out the loose boxes ready to leave for home. Issie tried to keep it together and return their friendly greetings and cries of congratulation, but although she managed to force a smile she was fighting to hold back the tears. It wasn't just the fact that Victory was one of her best horses. Or that she had been planning to prepare him for the Burghley Horse Trials in four months' time for the final phase of the Grand Slam. Issie's grief was more heartfelt. She adored the horse and couldn't bear the fact that her performance in the arena today would be the last time she'd ever ride him.

Victory was standing at the door of his stall when she arrived. The brown gelding let out a friendly nicker at the sight of her and Issie felt her heart breaking all over again. He had tried so hard for her in every way over the past three days. How was he to know that his incredible performance would actually mean he'd be taken away from her?

She reached out a hand to stroke his velvety muzzle.

"Hey, boy," she whispered softly. "You did real good out there today. I'm so proud of you. And I want you to know that this isn't my decision. But I can't stop…"

Victory suddenly jerked his head up. He could hear voices in the corridor. There were footsteps on the flagstones, coming their way. Issie looked up and saw Tulia Disbrowe walking with two men. She recognised one of them. He was a groom here at the stables and he carried a halter in his hand that was clearly intended for Victory. The other man was deep in conversation with Tulia. He was dressed in a sharp pinstripe suit, and Issie figured he must be the head of the syndicate.

There was something familiar about the other man. As he got closer he looked up the corridor and caught sight of Issie. He acknowledged her with a shark-like grin and in one crashing moment it dawned on Issie that she knew exactly who he was.

"Isadora," Tulia Disbrowe said. "I want you to meet the head of the syndicate…"

"We've met." Issie said flatly, cutting her short.

"Indeed we have," Oliver Tucker said, still maintaining his bone-chilling smile as he locked eyes with the girl in front of him. "Isadora and my daughter Natasha were at pony club together."

Tulia Disbrowe looked taken aback. "Well," she said, "isn't it a small world?"

"Way too small," Issie said darkly.

Clearly Tulia Disbrowe had no idea about the background of Victory's new owner. She didn't know that Oliver Tucker was a businessman who specialised in shady property deals – or that he had come unstuck when he had resorted to underhand tactics in his attempt to buy up the Chevalier Point Pony Club for redevelopment.

In the wake of the scandal and the lengthy investigations that had followed, Oliver Tucker had packed his bags and his family and left New Zealand for England. Despite his bankruptcy, Oliver Tucker had somehow managed to secrete away enough cash to buy a very nice mansion in Surrey. By all accounts the unscrupulous businessman still had many irons in the fire – including interests in the horse business.

The oily entrepreneur still seemed to be able to charm money out of people and he had the backing of a syndicate who, naturally, wanted nothing but the best. *Victory*. It must have given Oliver Tucker no end of pleasure to know that in buying this horse he had also managed to hurt Issie. Oliver Tucker had harboured a vicious grudge against her ever since Issie had blown the whistle on his Chevalier Point property scam. If Oliver Tucker was looking for revenge, there was no better way to exact it than by taking away her horse.

"Well, Tulia," Issie said, "I hope you realise that you've sold your horse to a bankrupt. The last time I heard,

Oliver was being investigated for fraud."

Oliver Tucker's smooth demeanour wasn't even ruffled.

"My personal wealth has nothing to do with this, Isadora," he said with a strained attempt at affability. "This is syndicate money that we're talking about. The investors who are backing me are the ones paying for the horse. I don't think Tulia will have any problem cashing her cheque."

All the same, Tulia pulled the cheque out of her pocket as he said this and looked at it rather anxiously. Issie ignored her.

"OK, Oliver," she said. "So you've bought the horse. Now what are you going to do with him?"

Oliver smirked at her. "I should have thought that was pretty clear. We're going to be competing him."

Issie gritted her teeth. "I meant who is going to be riding him?"

Oliver Tucker's mouth twisted up in a malevolent grin. "Haven't you figured it out yet?"

There were more footsteps behind Oliver Tucker, and a moment later a girl with glossy blonde hair, a deep orange tan and extremely purple jodhpurs appeared in the corridor.

"Dad!" she whined. "What's taking so long? Let's get the horse on the truck and go! Lance is waiting for me and I want to go to that party…"

The blonde girl stopped talking when she caught sight of Issie standing next to her father.

"Isadora," Oliver Tucker said, "I believe you know Victory's new rider? My daughter, Natasha Tucker."

While it was true that Oliver Tucker had kept a low profile since the Chevalier Point scandal, his daughter, Natasha, had done just the opposite. In fact, you would have needed to be living in a cave to avoid the stories about the bratty blonde.

In England, Natasha had quickly become a fixture on the posh party circuit with all the other young, spoilt and bored children of the rich and famous. It was at a party at the house of a pop star (or at least that's what the newspapers reported in the gossip pages) that Natasha met her new boyfriend, the famous footballer Lance Emmanuel.

A pasty-faced, thuggish lad, Lance was a gifted striker on a multi-million-pound contract with Chelsea.

As soon as she started dating Lance, paparazzi began following Natasha in the streets and hiding in the bushes outside the Tuckers' Surrey mansion.

Seizing the opportunity for fame, in a transformation that put Posh Spice and Cheryl Cole to shame, Natasha quickly added extensions to her already-long blonde hair, bought herself a lifetime ticket to 'Mahogany's Tanning Parlour' and promptly found herself a celebrity agent.

She began to develop a trademark fashion sense and whenever she left the house she was dressed in some bizarre concoction of Ugg boots and skimpy, fluffy purple clothing. She was constantly being photographed for the gossip pages that raved about her 'exotic style'.

Issie had laughed when she had read an interview with Natasha in the Daily Mail in which she had claimed that she had been a riding star back in her home country of New Zealand.

"Lance isn't the only one with sporting talent, you know," Natasha had told the reporter. "I've got my sights set on riding at the Olympics. All I need to do is find me the right horse."

At the time, Issie had thought that the comment was yet more typical pointless boasting. Even back at pony club Natasha had always made ridiculous claims that totally overstated her riding ability.

Now, of course, Issie realised that Natasha really did have plans to relaunch her riding career. She'd just been looking for the right horse. And now she had found him.

As the Badminton House groom entered the loose box to put the halter on Victory and lead him away, Natasha pushed her way past him.

"Oi!" she told the groom off. "I don't want that ugly halter!" She gestured in disgust at the elegant Kieffer leather halter that the groom had been about to slip over Victory's head.

Natasha reached into the glittery tote bag slung over her shoulder and pulled out her own halter instead. It was bright purple nylon with Swarovski crystals all over it and lilac hearts embroidered across the noseband.

"Ohmygod!" Issie stared at the awful halter in disbelief. Victory gave a horrified snort as Natasha lunged towards him with it, but he was too well-mannered to object as she shoved it on him.

"It's from my new collection," Natasha said proudly as she did up the buckle on the purple monstrosity. "I have my own clothing and horsewear brand – we do saddle blankets and rugs and jods. It's all purple and it has my initials on it."

Issie frowned. "Why would anyone want a saddle blanket with your initials?"

Natasha gave Issie a withering look. "Get a clue, Isadora! I've got it all – footballer boyfriend, my own equestrian fashion line, party invitations from pop stars. And in four months' time I'll be riding at the Burghley Horse Trials."

"You are kidding, right?" Issie couldn't take this any longer. "Natasha, it's not enough just to buy a good horse. You have to be able to ride it."

"I can ride," Natasha sniffed.

"Natasha, you don't get it," Issie was losing her cool. "This isn't a game. The cross-country course at Burghley is dangerous even for professionals. I've spent years working my way up to this, riding the international circuit in preparation."

Natasha's lips pursed like a cat's bottom. "You think you're just so special and fantastic, don't you, Isadora? Well, you're not. You won Badminton because you had a good horse – and now you're turning bitter and mean because I've taken him off you."

Issie was horrified. "Natasha! Be realistic! You've hardly ridden since pony club. Victory makes it look easy but he's a complicated ride…"

"For you maybe!" Natasha sneered. "But then I always was better than you. And now I'm going to prove it."

Natasha turned to her father. "OK, Dad. Let's go!"

Issie was exasperated. "Wait, Natasha. Listen, I can help you sort out his training schedule. You need to know about his feeding and his workouts and what tack we've been using…"

Natasha gave her a look of utter disinterest. "I've got staff for that sort of thing. I don't think we'll be needing your input, thanks very much."

And with that, she pushed past Issie. "See you at Burghley," she snapped.

Oliver Tucker gave Issie a look of triumph and strode off behind his daughter who was now leading Victory away up the corridor. Tulia Disbrowe had been watching the whole exchange between the two girls, and looked completely shell-shocked.

"I… I had no idea," she stammered. "I thought the syndicate was giving the ride to a seasoned professional."

"You had the right to sell him to whoever you wanted," Issie said. "Isn't that what you told me, Tulia? I hope the money makes you happy."

Tulia Disbrowe looked desperately apologetic, but there was nothing more she could say. She walked out of the stables alone, leaving Issie standing in the empty loose box.

In the next stall down, Nightstorm watched his stablemate leave and gave a distressed whinny, pacing up and down behind the bars of the loose box.

"Hey, Storm, it's OK." Issie unbolted the door to his box and walked inside so that she could reassure the stallion. "I'll miss him too, boy," she said, stroking his neck and whispering softly. "It's just you and me now."

At least the drama of Nightstorm's colic was over. The bay stallion was all she had left in the lead-up to Burghley.

CHAPTER 7

After Nightstorm's bout of colic, Issie was worried sick
that her horse would succumb to the dangerous condition
again. She had been nervous about transporting him back
from Badminton, fearing that the two-hour drive to
Wiltshire would stress him out and cause a relapse, but
Avery had reassured her. They left the estate grounds on
Monday afternoon, with Nightstorm travelling alone in
the massive horse truck now that his stablemate, Victory,
was gone.

When they arrived at The Laurels Issie decided it
would be best to box the stallion for the first night.
She was a little concerned that Storm would be anxious
about being left in his stall without another horse

beside him for company, but figured he would settle down eventually. After all, he'd been on his own in the stable for a night after Victory had gone and he'd been fine.

But Storm didn't settle this time. And the loose boxes at The Laurels were quite a different set-up to the ones at Badminton. Instead of having iron grilles on the top half of the door, they were open Dutch doors, with just a bottom half that secured the horse inside. Each stable had the same view, looking directly out at the fields. Issie figured that Nightstorm would be happy enough being able to stick his head out over the door and see the other horses out grazing nearby. And there was no way he could jump out since the Dutch doors were a substantial one metre-fifty in height.

She was wrong on both counts. Far from being content with his view, Nightstorm only became more agitated because he wanted to join them. And as for the height of a metre-fifty being enough to contain him, the big bay stallion disagreed.

Issie had left Nightstorm to eat his dinner and was sorting out the tack room when she heard a loud bang.

Nightstorm had been barging the stable door with his chest to push it down but the door was solid oak. When the barging tactic didn't work on the second try, the bay stallion turned around and went to the recesses of his box to get a run-up. If he couldn't force his way out, then he would jump it.

Issie emerged from the tack room just in time to catch sight of her horse flying through mid-air. He had his head down between his knees as he jumped so that he could squeak his way through the tiny gap between the door and the ceiling of the stable.

"Ohmygod, Storm! No!" Issie shouted at him but it was too late. Storm was already halfway over; his front legs had cleared the door and he had tucked up his back legs and managed to get them over as well. He landed on the other side of the box, took three strides and then dropped his head and began to graze contentedly. He didn't seem at all concerned about the fact that his hind leg had scraped the door as he went over, and there was now a strip of exposed flesh and blood oozing down his cannon bone.

"Ohmygod, Storm! What have you done?"

Feeling sick at the sight of the wound, Issie grabbed

a lead rope and clipped it onto his halter. The cut didn't look deep, but she would need to make him trot to find out if he was lame.

"Come on," Issie clucked with her tongue, asking the stallion to move forward. At a walk, Nightstorm seemed fine, but when he trotted her heart sank. He was definitely favouring the left hind.

Tying him up, Issie tried to move around the back and get a closer look at the wound, but Nightstorm wouldn't let her touch the leg. He kept kicking out every time she put her hand on it.

"Tom!" Issie tried shouting for help. "Stella?" There was no one else in the yard and it was almost dark. Issie knew that she had no choice. She would have to leave Nightstorm alone to get help.

She ran from the paddock to the house, adrenalin spurring her on.

Avery, Stella and Francoise were in the kitchen preparing dinner when she burst in.

"Isadora!" Francoise saw the panic written on her face. "What's happened?"

While Stella got out the emergency kit and Avery raced back down to the paddock with Issie, Francoise got straight on the phone to their vet, David White. Luckily, David was already on a call-out attending a broodmare at the farm just down the road and he made it over to The Laurels in a matter of minutes.

Issie, Avery, Francoise and Stella stood around watching in silence as the vet examined Nightstorm, who still wasn't keen on letting anyone touch the injured leg.

"Is it serious?" Issie asked.

"It looks like he might have damaged a tendon," David White said. "But I can't examine it with him moving around. I'll need to bring him into the clinic so that I can sedate him and clean and stitch the wound."

The trip to the vet was awful. Issie stayed in the back of the truck with Nightstorm, making sure that he didn't aggravate his injury. As she stood there stroking the stallion's muzzle and whispering to him softly, she kept going back over the events that had just happened. She should never have left the stallion in his box! If she could go back in time, she would. But the damage was done. It seemed incredible that on Sunday she had been looking to the future with two world-class eventers in her stables ready to ride at Burghley, and now, on Monday evening – she had none.

In the waiting room at the vet's clinic she paced the floor anxiously, unable to bring herself to sit down while David White and his team examined the horse.

The next half-hour seemed like an eternity and Issie was just about to barge her way into the operating theatre when David emerged through the surgery doors with good news.

"The tendon is lacerated but it's going to heal," he told her. "I've put four stitches in the leg near the hock and dressed the wound. You'll need to keep him on antibiotics to avoid infection – and he's on box rest for at least a month."

Issie was distraught. "But he'll make a full recovery after that?"

The vet nodded. "There's no reason why not. The tendon is still intact. But you'll have to bring him back into work slowly."

"He's due to compete at Burghley in August."

"Ah." The vet frowned. "Well, that will be touch and go. He might be well enough by then, or he might not.

I can't make you any promises at this stage, we'll have to see how he goes."

Back at The Laurels late that evening, Nightstorm was put back in the loose box. This time, however, he had another horse in the stall next door for company and he also had a makeshift grille of wooden bars blockading him in which Avery had hastily hammered into place.

"It's ironic," Stella said to Issie as they prepared his feed, "Storm tried to jump out of his box because he didn't want to be stuck in there – and now he's stuck in there for a whole month!"

"I don't think horses understand irony, Stella," Issie said.

"Neither do I really," Stella sighed. "But I'm pretty sure this qualifies."

That month was the very worst of times at The Laurels. Nightstorm hated being on box rest. The bay stallion was so fit and full of energy that he couldn't stand to be kept still all day and night and he didn't seem to accept that he was injured. He was in a sour, dejected mood and Issie would come away from her visits to his box feeling utterly miserable to see him in such a depressed state.

Issie returned to the house one morning after giving Nightstorm his breakfast and found Stella, Avery and Francoise at the kitchen table crowded around the morning paper laid out in front of them.

"Ohmygod!" Stella was saying. "I don't believe it!"

"What is it?" Issie asked innocently.

The others all turned around, startled.

"It's nothing!" Stella said hastily, trying to sneakily turn the page. "The usual rubbish. Nothing to see…"

"Stella?" Issie frowned. "Let me see the paper."

Stella shook her head. "Honestly, you don't need to read it, Issie," she insisted.

"Stella! Stop acting weird and give me the paper."

Issie made a swift grab and managed to wrench it out of Stella's hands.

She flipped the pages back to be greeted by an enormous photo of Natasha Tucker sitting astride Victory wearing her trademark purple jodhpurs and a self-satisfied grin. Beneath the picture was the headline *Victory for*

Natasha.

"What does that mean?" Issie frowned. "She hasn't actually won anything!"

Stella sighed. "You might as well read the story…"

Issie skimmed over the text beneath, eyes widening with every word.

Glamorous Natasha Tucker, girlfriend of footballer Lance Emmanuel, is back on track in her bid to compete at the Olympics – but first she has her sights set on winning the ultimate eventing competition – The Burghley Four-Star.

But the dedicated rider, who was a superstar back in New Zealand, is up against some nasty competition from the snobby equestrian world. Isadora Brown – a posh, top-class rider who has already won four-stars in Kentucky and at Badminton, has made no secret of her dislike for the lovely Natasha. The pair clashed publicly in the past and their rivalry has now reached fever pitch. Isadora is bitter and jealous that her former mount, Victory, has been snatched off her in favour of beautiful Natasha!

"This isn't professional – it's personal," a source close to both riders revealed to the Mail. "Their rivalry goes way back. Isadora is insanely jealous of Natasha."

Envious Isadora is also said to be furious at the success of Natasha's new fabulous equestrian clothing collection which features bright purple jodhpurs...

Issie couldn't read any more. She threw the newspaper across the kitchen in disgust.

"How can they publish that rubbish!" Issie was beside herself. "I'm not the posh one – she is! She used her father's money to take my horse off me!"

"Stay calm," Avery told Issie. "The papers don't know the real story. I'll give them a call straight away and we'll sort this out."

The next day, the Daily Mail arrived with another massive photo of Natasha and a new story on page five. This time the headline read: *Beautiful Natasha's Burghley dream – and the bitter pony-club instructor who wants to destroy it.*

If Natasha was the hero, then the newspapers needed a villain to pit her against and they had decided that Issie was perfect for the role. And with Lance Emmanuel in the middle of renegotiating a multi-million-pound contract with Chelsea, it seemed that no story about Lance and Natasha was too trivial to qualify as newsworthy.

Issie was horrified one morning when she popped out to get some milk and discovered paparazzi photographers lurking in wait for her! Natasha, on the other hand, was clearly lapping up the attention. Every day there seemed to be a picture of her at some new event, and the papers were filled with images of the bratty blonde posing like a Hollywood superstar on the red carpet.

The stories that really drove Issie bonkers were the ones that focused on Natasha's preparations for Burghley. Apparently she was sparing no expense for the competition.

Stella, who had her ear to the ground with the grooms at the other stables around the district, was the one that discovered just how star-studded Team Natasha had become.

"She's employed the world's best showjumper, Hans Shockelmann, to give her lessons!" Stella told Issie incredulously, "Plus, I heard from Louise down at the Goldin stables that Natasha's also got the gold medallist Arianna O'Hurley to give her dressage instruction twice a day! I wouldn't be surprised if she's booked Lucinda Green to train her for cross-country!"

Avery wasn't perturbed. "She could hire the entire British equestrian team for all the good it will do her," he harrumphed. "You can't become good enough in four months to ride at the Burghley Horse Trials!"

"I don't know." Issie looked doubtful. "I mean, Hans and Arianna are totally amazing world-class riders…"

"…and Natasha is not," Avery said bluntly. "She's a fake and everyone will soon realise that."

For once, however, Avery was completely wrong. No one seemed to realise that Natasha wasn't the superstar she was making herself out to be. Two weeks after the story of Natasha taking over the ride on Victory had broken, another nasty piece ran in which they pitted the two girls as arch-rivals. The new story claimed that Issie was so afraid to clash head-on with Natasha she had thrown a colossal tantrum and refused to compete Storm at the upcoming Luhmuhlen horse trials.

Issie was devastated. It was true that she wouldn't be riding at Luhmuhlen – but that was because Storm's injury wouldn't be healed in time.

"No one will believe their story," Avery said.

But the mud was clearly starting to stick. A day later

The Laurels received a rather unexpected email from Dashing Equine, Issie's major sponsor. Their financial support had been a godsend and literally saved the farm after Issie won at Kentucky. They had offered Issie a lucrative sum in exchange for being the face of their brand. But now, according to the email from the company, there had been a 'change of direction' and they 'no longer wanted to continue the relationship'. Neither did Issie's other biggest sponsor, GG Feeds, who also sent an email telling her that they were withdrawing their support.

"Cowards and opportunists!" Avery fumed when Issie came into the kitchen and showed him the email that morning. "They were happy to have their brand names plastered all over you when things were going well, but the minute times get tough, they're gone! They didn't even have the decency to front up and tell us in person."

"They didn't need to tell us," Stella said. "I think we would have figured it out once we saw this!" She held up the morning's paper. This time the massive photo of Natasha was taken in front of a Dashing Equine horse truck — and in her hands Natasha held a huge bag of

GG horse feed.

"This can't really be happening!" Issie groaned, slumping down at the kitchen table. The vet bills for Nightstorm's recovery from the stall injury were adding up fast. Victory was gone and now so were the sponsors. At this rate they would barely have enough cash in the coffers to pay the Burghley entry fee – even if Nightstorm had recovered in time.

"We need to keep calm," Avery was saying as he made himself a cup of tea. "Perhaps it's worth trying to talk to the sponsors…"

A knock at the door put an end to the conversation.

"Are we expecting someone?" Francoise asked suspiciously.

"Maybe we shouldn't answer it," Stella said. "It could be the paparazzi. I saw a photographer outside the front gates today."

Issie stood up from the table. "Well, if it is a photographer, I'll just tell them to go away."

Things were getting crazy, but Issie wasn't going to start living in fear of answering her own front door! She walked down the hallway, trying to make out the figure that she could see on the other side of the opaque glass.

Taking a deep breath, she turned the knob and opened the door.

Standing on the doorstep was a boy in dark blue denim jeans and a white T-shirt. He looked almost as surprised to see Issie as she was to see him.

"Oh good!" He looked relieved. "When I saw the paparazzi I thought I'd turned up at Lady Gaga's country house by mistake!" He smiled. "Well, Issie, aren't you going to ask me in?"

Standing on Issie's doorstep was Marcus Pearce.

CHAPTER 8

The last person in the world Issie had expected to see was Marcus.

"You can't be here!" Issie blurted out. "You're supposed to be in America!"

Marcus laughed, "You're not pleased to see me?"

"No," Issie stammered, "I mean, yes, of course I am! But I thought you were working for the Valmont Stables out in California?"

"I quit," Marcus shrugged. "Things kind of fell apart after all the drama at Kentucky. I turned up for work one morning and the head of the stables told me that they were planning to sell Liberty. I figured there was no point in sticking around if they were going to sell my best horse out from under me, so I resigned."

He looked at Issie. "I hear you've been having similar problems of your own?"

"You could say that," Issie replied gazing at this handsome boy with the honey-blond hair and green eyes who had turned up out of nowhere.

"Why are you looking at me like that?" Marcus asked.

"I still can't believe you're actually here."

"Is that why you haven't asked me to come in?" Marcus grinned.

"Oh!" Issie realised that they were still standing on the doorstep. "Come in. Everyone's in the kitchen and I think there's still some bacon and eggs left if you're hungry…"

Avery, Stella and Francoise were just as shocked as Issie to see Marcus. Cups of tea were brewed, breakfast was dished up and Marcus filled them all in on what had happened to him since the Kentucky Four-Star. It turned out that he had only told Issie half the story.

"The day that I resigned I had no idea what I was going to do, and totally no plan," Marcus told them as he bit into his toast. "Then I get this phone call out of the blue saying that Gerhardt Muller had been injured on the cross-country at Badminton and did I want to take over the ride on Velluto Rosso?" Marcus lifted up his left arm and Issie saw that it was no longer in a plaster cast. "My arm had healed up by then and I was ready to ride, and Gerhardt is a friend of mine so of course I said yes. Then they told me that the horse was based at the Goldin Farm in Wiltshire. So here I am – back in England for the first time since I left home for Blainford Academy!"

It was a fantastic story. And yet, Issie found herself slightly disappointed by it. She'd been half expecting Marcus to say that he had come all the way to the UK to turn up and surprise her. Hearing that he was in the neighbourhood anyway was strangely a bit of a let-down.

"So, it looks like Issie and I are both going to be riding at Burghley," Marcus said cheerfully. Then he saw the long faces around the kitchen table.

"What's the matter? Did I say something wrong?"

"It's Storm," Issie told him. "He's had an accident. I don't know if I'm going to be riding at all."

After breakfast, Issie took Marcus down to the stables to meet Nightstorm.

"He injured himself three weeks ago," she explained as they walked down the driveway. "The wound has healed up nicely and he's only got another week on box rest. Then I'm allowed to bring him slowly back into work."

Marcus frowned, "You'll have a lot of ground to make up," he said. "A month in the box will mean his muscles are wasted. I see what you mean about cutting it fine for Burghley."

Issie nodded. "Tom has worked out a training schedule. It's going to be tight but I think we'll have him ready. As long as the leg holds out…"

Issie led the way along the row of loose boxes. In the second-to-last box she had stabled a black gelding called Bonaparte to keep Storm company. Bonaparte stuck his head out and nickered to her when she arrived.

"Is this him?" Marcus asked.

Issie shook her head. She gave a whistle and a moment later, in the box next to Bonaparte's a striking bay stallion stuck his head over the door.

"This is Nightstorm," Issie said, reaching a hand up to stroke the stallion's broad white blaze.

"Wow," Marcus looked genuinely impressed. "He's really something, isn't he?"

"I think so," Issie said, looking doe-eyed at her horse. "I've known him from the moment he was born. His mother was my old pony-club mare and his sire was one of the dressage stallions from El Caballo Danza Magnifico."

"With bloodlines like that he must be pretty good at dressage, then?" Marcus asked.

Issie sighed. "Yes – and no. Storm is capable of pulling out a great test, but he's unpredictable. Five minutes before we entered the arena at Badminton he'd actually just bucked me off! I got lucky and he behaved himself after that, but I need to figure out a way to make sure he'll always perform – to get some certainty with him, you know?"

"I know," Marcus agreed. "The best ones are always so complicated." He reached up to stroke Nightstorm's muzzle, and Issie could see the genuine love and understanding of horses that he possessed.

"Do you want a tour of the rest of the stables?" she asked.

As they walked around the yards, Issie filled Marcus

in on everything that had happened over the past months since they'd last seen each other. The loss of Victory to Natasha Tucker and the fickle departure of Issie's sponsors left him stunned.

"Even with all of those trainers working for her, she'll never get up to speed for Burghley," Marcus concluded. "Not if she's never ridden a four-star course before."

Issie wasn't so sure. "She's going to ride Victory at the Luhmuhlen Horse Trials as a warm-up. Apparently – according to the papers – I'm too chicken to face her!"

Luhmuhlen was a famous four-star eventing track in Germany. The timing of the event meant that many of the top UK-based riders used Luhmuhlen as a test run for Burghley.

"It'll be my first competition on Velluto Rosso," Marcus told her. "If you can't face Natasha then I'll do it for you."

"So why exactly did Marcus Pearce drop by?" Stella asked when they were all sitting down to dinner that evening.

Issie kept her eyes on her plate, "I don't know. He was in the neighbourhood, I guess, so he came to say hi."

"The Goldin Stables aren't exactly 'in the neighbourhood'," Stella said doing air quotes. "They're about twenty kilometres away."

"He was just being polite," Issie said.

Stella gave a smirk at the stiffness of Issie's reply. "He likes you!"

Issie could feel herself blushing. "He's just a friend," she said. "And he's leaving for Germany at the end of the week and by the time he gets back we'll both be frantic in the lead-up to Burghley…"

Issie had a training schedule and it didn't leave any time for boys – not even a boy like Marcus Pearce.

She didn't see Marcus again before he left for Luhmuhlen. She did get a text a couple of weeks later saying that Velluto Rosso had travelled fine in the horse truck to Germany, and that the chestnut mare had settled in well.

Issie had read the papers that weekend hoping that, since Marcus was riding for Great Britain, there might be news on how he was doing. But the only stories were about Natasha Tucker.

The writers in The Sun's sports section had a field day over the so-called scandal when Natasha was banned from wearing her trademark bright purple jodhpurs to ride her dressage test.

"Uptight equestrians!" one Sun columnist opined. "Stop being prissy and let smasher Natasha wear purple pants!"

Had things really been reduced to this? Who cared what colour jodhpurs Natasha wore?

"Actually," Stella said when she read the article, "I quite like those purple jods she wears."

Issie looked at her dumbfounded.

"What?" Stella said. "I like purple, OK? In fact, I even think a colourful halter can look kind of cute on the right pony. It doesn't mean I like Natasha – obviously."

"Purple jods are so not the point," Issie said. "I'm just sick of them running news stories about her like she's a proper rider."

"Well it can't go on for much longer," Stella said. "Tomorrow in the dressage arena they're going to finally see the truth."

Stella's prediction was startling accurate. It didn't matter how many expensive trainers and minions Natasha employed, they couldn't paper over the cracks in her performance. Her test at Luhmuhlen was nothing short of a disaster. From the moment Natasha Tucker bumbled into the dressage arena in a disunited canter and made a ham-fisted salute to the judges she proceeded to massacre every single movement. Her final dressage score was the worst on record at Luhmuhlen since the event began.

Rumour had it that Natasha threw such a brat fit backstage afterwards that not one but two of her world-famous instructors quit on the spot.

Natasha went into the cross-country the next day at the bottom of the rankings on a stonking score of eighty-five points. As it happened, her atrocious dressage score hardly mattered. Her cross-country was so bad she was eliminated at fence number two when Victory refused point-blank to jump.

Two refusals was enough to get her eliminated at Luhmuhlen and Natasha was forced to make the walk of shame back to the start of the course. There, she caused a total scene by turning her wrath on the remaining members of her training team who were still on speaking terms with her.

All of this gossip was gleaned second-hand via Stella from the grooms who worked the circuit at Luhmuhlen. According to them, the worst part was the fact that the rest of the syndicate members who owned Victory were right there watching the whole drama.

Eliminated from the competition, Natasha didn't even stay on at Luhmuhlen to watch the showjumping the next day. If she had stayed, she would have seen one of the most closely-fought contests in the history of three-day eventing as the six leading riders came into the ring with less than ten points separating them. In the end, the winner of Luhmuhlen, with a dressage score of 38, and two incredible clear rounds, was the UK's Marcus Pearce on Velluto Rosso.

Meanwhile, back at The Laurels, Nightstorm was finally allowed out from enforced box rest. Issie had started his rehabilitation by taking him for gentle half-hour hacks each day along the bridlepaths on the property. This was trickier than it sounded since Nightstorm, bored and restless after a whole month trapped in the loose box, was highly-strung and mad keen for a gallop. He didn't take kindly to the fact that Issie was insistent that he stay at a walk the whole time.

By the end of the first week, Issie's arm muscles ached from holding the stallion back, and she was relieved when David White popped around for a check-up and declared that she could now include some trot and canter work in Storm's programme.

"No arena work yet though," David had clarified. "It's too tough on the legs."

Far from being frustrated, Issie was relieved to have an excuse to avoid the dressage arena. The Badminton Horse Trials had been a lucky fluke. The stallion remained unpredictable and headstrong – and Issie had no idea what to do about it.

She needed to find a new approach – and she needed to find it soon. Nightstorm's leg was almost healed and when the vet gave him the all clear she would need to begin dressage training in earnest. It was already July so there were only two months left before Burghley.

One evening, Issie called a meeting with Stella, Avery and Francoise in the hope that the four of them could figure out a solution to the dressage problem.

"We could try drugging him," Stella suggested.

"And end up getting disqualified for using illegal substances," Avery said.

"No," Stella said. "There are loads of drugs that are totally legal to use. We could give him Steady Neddy, it's herbal and it calms them right down."

Issie shook her head, "I don't think making him dozy is the answer."

Francoise looked thoughtful. "Storm is a very smart horse, maybe we need to make things harder for him?"

"What do you mean?" Issie asked.

"An eventing dressage test is very simple in many ways," Francoise explained. "There is no piaffe, no passage. Storm has El Caballo bloodlines, which means he is capable of learning far more complex high school manoeuvres like courbettes and caprioles. If all we ask him to do is an extended trot and a half-pass there's no challenge in it for him. He acts up because he is bored."

The others all agreed that the theory could be true.

"So what's the answer?" Issie said.

Francoise paused and then she said. "We train him

in the dressage arena as if he were an El Caballo performing stallion."

Issie was confused. "But he's not going to be required to perform any of the high school movements at Burghley – it's a waste of time!"

"No," Francoise said. "It's not. The point is to keep him thinking. If his brain is busy he will no longer buck out of boredom."

Issie could see that the idea would work for the schooling sessions. "But it's only a temporary solution. At some stage we have to stop doing fancy leaps and start learning the actual dressage test – and then he'll get bored and throw a bucking fit – possibly in the arena at Burghley."

Francoise frowned. "I have not got the answer for you yet when it comes to the competition itself," she said. "Hopefully, we will solve that problem too before Burghley."

The weeks of July were already flying by and Nightstorm was getting fitter by the day. The kilos that the stallion had gained from his weeks of being immobilised were quickly lost as Issie stepped up his training and began to take him out every other day for gallop sessions up the big hill track at the back of The Laurels.

On alternate days, she would school the stallion over showjumps or in the dressage arena and so far she had to admit that Francoise's outlandish training suggestion was definitely working.

Now that Nightstorm was being challenged by the *haute école* moves, he no longer threw hissy fits or got stroppy. He was a remarkably quick study, and within a couple of sessions he had mastered the capriole, one of the most complex 'airs above ground', rising up on his hindquarters and leaping off the ground so that he seemed to float in mid-air, before kicking out his hind legs.

Issie was amazed at how quickly the skills that she had learnt under Roberto Nunez's tutelage when she rode at El Caballo Danza Magnifico all came rushing back to her. With Francoise on hand to assist her, Issie was able to train Nightstorm as if he too were one of El Caballo's flying stallions – which, in a way, he was, since he was descended directly from the great Marius himself.

One afternoon Issie and Francoise were in the arena schooling Nightstorm to perform the courbette, a move in which the horse reared up and stayed balanced on its hind legs before bouncing forward like a bunny hopping.

It was a precarious and dangerous task learning this movement. If the stallion reared up too far and lost his balance he could go over backwards. For the rider, the move required utmost precision. Issie was so focused on what she was doing that she didn't notice that they had an audience. While she had been training, a silver Lexus had eased up their driveway and parked right beside the arena.

"Were you expecting company?" Francoise asked.

Issie looked over at the Lexus. It had tinted windows, making it impossible to see who was inside. The car sat there for a moment idling, and then the engine was switched off, and the driver got out. The chauffeur was dressed in the traditional uniform of a black suit and cap and he scurried around the car and ran to open the back door for his VIP passenger. As the door swung open Issie couldn't believe her eyes.

"Oh, you're kidding me! What does he want now?"

Full of bravado, Oliver Tucker emerged from his Lexus and strutted towards the arena. Issie couldn't believe it when Tucker gave her a cheery wave as if they were old friends. But things were about to become even stranger still. Oliver Tucker was about to make her an offer that she couldn't refuse.

CHAPTER 9

Oliver Tucker surveyed his surroundings, running a property developer's eye over the stable blocks and fields.

"Nice set-up you've got here, Isadora," he said. "Very pleasant indeed."

"What do you want, Oliver?" Issie said nervously. The last time she'd seen this man he'd taken her horse away. She didn't trust him as far as she could throw him – and she certainly didn't like the way he was looking around The Laurels as if he owned the place.

"There's no need to be rude," Oliver Tucker smiled his shark grin at her. "I've come here with a business proposition for you, young lady, so it would be in your best interests to use your manners and invite me in for a cup of tea."

Issie stood her ground. "I'm busy, Oliver. If you want to talk to me then do it here. I have horses to ride."

"I'm sure you do," Oliver Tucker said. "So how would you like one more?"

"What are you talking about?" Issie said.

Oliver Tucker cleared his throat. "I have come to make you an offer on behalf of the syndicate. We'd like you to ride one of our horses in the Burghley Horse Trials."

Issie was as stunned as a mullet. "You're kidding me!"

Oliver Tucker's face was expressionless. "I can assure you that I'm not," he replied. "The offer is quite genuine. The syndicate is willing to pay you handsomely to take over the ride and prepare the horse over the next four weeks in time for the competition…"

Issie shook her head. "Tell your syndicate no, thank you. I'm not interested in a chance ride on some unproven horse…"

"You misunderstand me," Oliver Tucker interrupted her. "You've already ridden this horse before."

Issie's eyes widened as she realised what Oliver Tucker was driving at. "That's right," he said. "I'm offering you the ride on Victory."

"I can't believe it!" Avery was incredulous, "After everything he's done, Oliver Tucker has the bare-faced cheek to turn up and ask you to ride for him?"

"He didn't have much of a choice," Issie said. "Oliver acts like he's in charge but really it's the syndicate who actually own Victory. They had a complete wig-out when Natasha failed so badly at Luhmuhlen and demanded that he swap back to letting me ride him."

"It's true," Stella came into the kitchen to join them. "I just got a call from a friend of mine who works at Ravenshead Park where Natasha has been keeping Victory. She said Natasha was given a second chance by the syndicate after Luhmuhlen. They gave her a month to pull herself together and get Victory back on track. She went into total overdrive with her trainers trying to fix the problems but last weekend at a two-star competition at Blair Castle Natasha got the worst dressage mark again – and was eliminated on the cross-country – again. At that point, the syndicate decided that they couldn't possibly let her ride the horse at Burghley."

Avery shook his head in amazement. "So Oliver Tucker took the horse back off his own daughter and offered the ride to you? Good gravy! That man would sell his grandmother if there was cash in it."

Issie looked at her instructor. "So what do you think? Are we taking him up on it?"

"I don't know," Avery said. "Getting involved with Oliver Tucker is a risky business…"

"But it's worth the risk, isn't it? If it means that Issie can ride Victory at Burghley," Stella said.

"I don't trust Tucker either," Issie agreed. "But I don't see how he can wiggle out of it once the deal is done. The names of the riders for Burghley have to be confirmed tomorrow."

Avery considered this.

"I still think Tucker is as dodgy as a three-pound note… but it's too good an opportunity to pass up."

"You're right," Issie agreed.

"Well, that settles it." Stella stood up from the table.

"I guess I'll go and get a stable ready for Victory!"

"Are you sure you want to do this, Issie?" Avery looked worried.

Issie nodded. "Make the phone call, Tom. Tell Tucker that we're in."

As soon as she was alone Issie realised the enormity of what she had just agreed to. Victory was coming home. And now she would be riding two horses at Burghley after all.

Oliver Tucker didn't return to The Laurels again. He sent a couple of his minions to drop the horse off the next morning in the Ravenshead Park truck. As the men unloaded the brown gelding, Issie's heart leapt. It was so good to have him back!

Avery, however, wasn't smiling at the sight of the horse. Instead, he was casting a critical eye over Victory. He looked to be in fair health – but to be ready for Burghley in four weeks his condition had to be assessed and perfected as if he were an Olympic athlete.

"He's carrying too much weight," Avery said. "Look at the barrel on him! He looks more like a show pony than a three-day eventer!"

Stella agreed. "I'll put him on a new feed regime straight away. He needs to drop twenty kilos or he'll never make it around the track at Burghley under the time."

Avery watched his wife as she ran her hands over the horse, checking for injuries. "Any problems, Francoise?"

Francoise spent a little longer examining Victory's legs. "He seems sound enough, no scrapes or splints, but look here on his rump how he has lost muscle tone! He's obviously been spending all his time in the dressage arena. We need to start doing more hill training and gallops to build his stamina," Francoise frowned. "It worries me, Tom, he has lost so much fitness I am not certain that I can get him ready for Burghley…"

Issie looked on as her team discussed Victory's conditioning schedule. It was at moments like this that she realised just how incredibly lucky she was to have these three people on her side. Francoise had the most amazing intuition when it came to choosing the training format for each individual horse. It was almost like she was a horse herself, the way she understood their needs and their bodies so perfectly. And when it came to stabling and feeding, there was no one in the game better than Stella. Issie's best friend might act goofy and silly but she was deadly serious about her professional work and had an encyclopaedic knowledge of horse feeds and supplements.

And then there was Tom. Even after all these years, Issie still found herself in awe at the depth of his knowledge and experience. In the final weeks before Burghley, Avery's own experiences as a professional rider would be invaluable. He knew exactly what the challenges would be and how to prepare Issie and her horses to tackle them.

"The chief factor that separates Burghley from Badminton is the cross-country course," Avery told Issie as they walked Victory towards the stables. "Burghley is a tougher course in many ways. The terrain is undulating, with lots of hills and valleys, so it's very demanding on the horses. Nightstorm is recovering well from his leg injury and I'm confident we can get him back to peak fitness, but it will be touch-and-go whether

Victory will be ready to tackle it."

He turned to Issie. "You'll need to be at peak fitness too, if you're going to be riding two horses around the course. I think a little bit of extra training might be required."

Issie had assumed that he meant galloping – or maybe cross-country training. But Avery explained that the sort of work he had in mind didn't involve horses at all.

"Be at the stables at six a.m. tomorrow," he told her. "And wear your trainers and a track suit. We're going jogging."

Issie had always considered herself to be pretty athletic. After all, she was in the saddle for at least three or four hours every day. She'd never had any trouble bringing a horse home on the cross-country course before. But with the very last phase of the Grand Slam looming Avery wasn't taking any chances with her fitness levels.

"This will be your new routine in the lead-up to Burghley. You're going to be running ten kilometres every morning from now until the competition begins,"

Avery told her when they met up at the stables that morning.

"Ten kilometres!" Issie was shocked. "That'll take forever!"

Avery looked at the watch on his wrist. "No, it won't," he said firmly. "Because I'll be riding alongside and timing you. I expect you to complete ten kilometres in under an hour."

"This isn't fair! Why do you get to ride?" Issie groaned as they set off down the driveway of The Laurels with Avery on Bonaparte.

Avery ignored her complaints and began to talk tactics as Issie puffed away alongside him. For the hour that she ran, he walked and trotted the horse steadily to keep pace with her, all the while telling her about the things she would need to know to master the cross-country course at Burghley.

"Delaney Swift is the course designer this year," Avery reminded her, "and she's bound to include lots of corners – she always does. We'll have to practise those at home. Delaney is also famous for her dramatic water jumps so I expect the water complex to be tough this year. You'll be fine in the water on Victory but you'll have to keep a tight hold on Nightstorm. He's too brave for his own good and tends to rush his jumps. If he charges into the lake you'll end up splashing, which can be blinding for both of you…"

This one-sided conversation became a regular part of their morning schedule over the next few weeks. At first, Issie found the morning jogs utterly unbearable and felt like her lungs would burst or her legs would give out. But within a fortnight she discovered what joggers refer to as a 'runner's high'. After the first two or three kilometres she would feel a surge of adrenalin and from there she would begin to power into the run, really pumping her arms and legs so that Avery would be forced to raise the pace of Bonaparte's trot to keep up. Very soon Issie found that she could modulate her breathing so that she could actually speak comfortably to Avery as she ran, and with this newfound skill she began asking crucial questions about the best way to ride both of her horses.

The theory she learnt on the morning runs was tested each day on the cross-country course. Avery had constructed a series of fences around the perimeter of The Laurels. Here they would practise various combinations of ditches, coffins, staircases and banks, preparing Issie for any eventuality and showing her the pitfalls and possible mistakes she might make. During these sessions Issie began to understand just how much she still had to learn – and how much Avery could still teach her.

"Do you think I'll still be having lessons with you when I'm, like, fifty?" Issie asked with a grin.

"I hope so," Avery replied. "The best riders keep on improving. Only the foolish ones think that they have nothing left to learn."

Each afternoon, after exhausting herself over fences under Avery's tuition, Issie would mount up on her alternate ride and head into the dressage arena for schooling with Francoise.

Issie honestly couldn't figure out how Natasha had managed to do so badly in her dressage tests since Victory was a dream ride who never put a hoof wrong. Nightstorm, on the other hand, continued to be erratic. The stallion's schooling sessions usually went brilliantly during the warm-up phase and then after the first fifteen or twenty minutes he would begin a petulant bucking fit right in the middle of a flying change or a passage.

"He is fine until he decides that he has done enough for one day, and then he explodes," Francoise summed up. She was forced to admit that she still didn't know what to do about it.

Adding further to their training issues, Francoise seemed to have succumbed to the flu. It was only one week to the horse trials now, but Francoise felt so ill that she had to stay in bed, leaving Issie to school Nightstorm on her own.

One day the session without Francoise was particularly disastrous. Things started out OK. In fact, Nightstorm was totally brilliant for the first fifteen minutes. But when Issie attempted to run through the dressage test, it all came unstuck. When Nightstorm began to fuss over doing the flying changes across the arena, Issie became insistent, and that was when the stallion's temper flared. Nightstorm dumped her on the sand surface of the arena not once, but twice! In the end, they finished the schooling session with Issie in tears of rage, and Nightstorm resembling a dragon more than a horse, red-eyed with nostrils wide and ears flat back in anger.

Issie and the stallion weren't on speaking terms as she led him back to his stable. This was a nightmare! She had always imagined that she had a special relationship with Storm. She had been through so much with this horse to get this far. She had travelled to the other side of the world to win him back in a Spanish street race. She had put herself through the rigours of learning the *haute école* from El Caballo Danza Magnifico to win their approval and take him home. Under her care, the colt had grown and blossomed into an incredible horse. And yet, even though Storm adored her, he still fought against her. She knew that he had the talent to win at Burghley. So why was it that instead of bringing the best out in her horse in the dressage arena, she always seemed to lock horns with him? She felt like it was her fault that they kept fighting but she had no idea how to stop the stallion's temper tantrums.

Back at the stables, still in a black mood, she unsaddled Storm and went to put away his tack. By the time she came back to the box Stella was there, brushing the stallion down.

"I've got his feed ready," Stella said. "I'll just rug him up and..." Then she saw the tears in Issie's eyes, and the miserable expression on her best friend's face.

"Issie? What's wrong?"

"He bucked me off again," Issie admitted. "Twice."

"Oh." Stella put down the brushes. "Are you OK?"

Issie brushed the tears away angrily with her hand. She was a professional rider – it was stupid to be crying about this! But with only a week to go she was feeling totally desperate and she had run out of ideas and excuses.

"There was no reason for it," Issie shook her head. "He was perfect when we were warming up. And then about twenty minutes into the ride he just threw a fit and I ended up on the ground."

Issie looked at Storm. "He hates the dressage arena – and sometimes I think he hates me for making him go in there."

"Well, he doesn't totally hate it," Stella said. "He likes the first fifteen minutes. It's a shame that you're not riding a warm-up at Burghley – then he'd be fantastic!"

"Ohmygod!" Issie froze.

"What?" Stella said. "Is something wrong?"

"No!" Issie squealed. "You're totally right! That's it! That's the solution. Ohmygod! Stella, you are a total genius!"

"I am?" Stella looked even more confused. "Uhhh, are you going to tell me why?"

"Come on!" Issie could barely contain her excitement. "Give Storm his feed and then we'll go and find Tom and Francoise – they need to hear this!"

Stella had just given Issie the answer she had been looking for. Suddenly, she knew exactly what to do to get the best performance out of her stallion in the dressage arena at Burghley. With just one week to go until the three-day event began, she finally had a plan.

CHAPTER 10

In the final week of the lead-up to Burghley, preparations were intense.

There was so much to organise. The tack and equipment had to be prepped and packed in the truck by Wednesday ready for the trip to Lincolnshire. With so many details to organise, Avery called a planning meeting in the kitchen on Sunday morning and that was when Stella dropped her bombshell.

"I think you should hire another groom," she told them.

Issie couldn't believe it. "You're quitting?"

"No!" Stella rolled her eyes. "Of course not! But I don't think I can handle two different horses on the day. I know you're the one who's actually riding, but there's so much to organise behind the scenes and I don't want to make a mistake. I feel like I'll be spreading myself too thin if I look after Storm and now Victory as well. We need a second back-up groom to take over one of your mounts."

"Well, it's a bit late to think of it now!" Avery pointed out. "We've got less than a week before Burghley begins – all the best grooms in the UK will already be locked in with other stables. How are we possibly going to get someone we can trust to do the job at such short notice?"

Issie and Stella looked at each other and smiled. They both had exactly the same idea.

"The best grooms in the UK might have jobs already," Issie replied, "but there's one in New Zealand who might be available."

It was nine in the evening in Chevalier Point when the phone rang at Kate Knight's house. She assumed the call would be one of her pony-club kids calling to ask about the rally tomorrow. The last thing she'd been expecting was a job offer from an old friend on the other side of the world.

"Kate," Issie said, "I know it's, like, super-short notice and everything, but I somehow ended up with another horse to ride at Burghley and Stella can't cope and…"

"Hey! Issie!" Kate interrupted her friend in mid-babble. "You don't have to explain. If you need me then I'm totally there. Just tell me what flight to catch and I'll start packing my bags."

It was a typical Kate reaction and Issie realised just how much they needed her. Always the calm, collected one – Kate was the best possible person to have on your team when the pressure was on.

Issie remembered so clearly that day at Pony Club when she had met Kate for the first time. Kate had a horse called Toby, a full-sized hack that towered over Stella and Issie's ponies. Kate towered over them too – she was a year older than Stella and Issie and had a leggy physique and Nordic blonde hair.

The three girls were so different physically. Alongside cool, blonde Kate there was no way that Stella with her out-of-control red curls and Issie with her long, dark hair could ever have been mistaken for sisters. But they certainly felt like a family. As Issie's mum had often pointed out, deep down they were all cut from the same cloth – totally horse-mad.

Years had passed and distance had separated the girls but their mutual love of horses had never faded. When Issie and Stella had moved to England to focus on riding the international eventing circuit, Kate had chosen to stay in Chevalier Point where she had taken over Avery's old job as the head instructor at the Pony Club, while studying full-time to become a vet.

Kate had never been to The Laurels before now. But from the moment she arrived, jet-lagged, off the flight from New Zealand, it was as if she had been a part of the team there forever.

There was little time for emotional reunions and the girls got straight down to business. It was already Tuesday. The horse truck was pre-loaded with their kit and the girls and Avery planned to rise at five and depart by six the next morning for Burghley.

"You're being assigned Victory and I'll take care of Storm," Stella told Kate. "Come down to the stables and I'll explain the feeding schedules and his tack. We'll work together to prepare both the horses for competition.

The first trot-up is early on Thursday morning – the day after tomorrow. Then the dressage begins on Friday…"

"Wow," Kate took a deep breath. "Thrown straight in at the deep end! I haven't groomed for anyone in years, you do realise?"

"You'll be fine!" Issie insisted. "Stella is totally organised and she'll show you the ropes."

"We're glad to have you aboard," Avery confirmed. "It will be good to have a vet on the team."

"Hey!" Kate said. "I'm only in my second year! I'm not a qualified vet yet!"

"Come on," Stella told her, "I'll take you down to the stables now and you can meet Victory."

At 5.45 the next morning the girls loaded the two horses into their individual bays in the back of the horse truck and then they piled into the cabin in the mid-section ready to depart for Lincolnshire.

"Where's Avery?" Stella said looking at her watch anxiously.

"He's saying goodbye to Francoise," Issie said.

There was too much going on at The Laurels for the Frenchwoman to abandon the farm and come along too. It was foaling season, and they were expecting a very special new addition to the stables at The Laurels as part of their new sporthorse breeding programme. A year ago Francoise had purchased a stunning broodmare, a pretty chestnut called Mirabelle. The mare was now heavily in foal to a famous warmblood stallion called Miracle Maker and she was expected to give birth that week.

Plus there were three up-and-coming young eventers who were currently in work being prepared for a novice competition next month. And Francoise was still under the weather. Her flu appeared to be lingering and she was frequently feeling queasy in the mornings.

Issie was reluctant to leave Francoise behind, but the dressage trainer had dismissed her fears. "When you told me your plan for handling Nightstorm at Burghley I knew that you understood this horse better than anyone," Francoise told Issie. "You are ready to do this on your own."

"No! I need you there!" Issie insisted.

The French trainer shook her head. "Isadora, I have

taught you everything that I know. When dressage day comes at Burghley it is you and you alone who will take the horses into that arena. I cannot go in there with you. In the end, it will be up to you."

And so it was that the team who departed that morning was the same team that Issie remembered from her days back home at Chevalier Point. With Avery at the wheel of the truck and her two best and oldest friends beside her, Issie set off on the journey towards Lincolnshire, on her way to the three-day event that would define her riding career forever.

In the sport of three-day eventing there were only six events in the whole world that classified for the highest challenge level – the four-star event.

Competitors would often debate which of the four-stars was the greatest of them all. The top two were without a doubt the Badminton Horse Trials and the Burghley Horse Trials, held in the grand grounds of the Burghley Estate, with its glorious gardens and elegant Elizabethan palace.

"Back in my day," Avery said as he drove the truck through the gates of Burghley, "there was no debate. Without question, Badminton was considered the tougher test. The fences were more complex, the competition was stiffer..."

Avery parked the truck under an enormous spreading oak tree and turned to Issie. "But these days I would rate Burghley as its equal – the pinnacle of competition. The very best riders come here to compete and the cross-country course is arguably tougher than even Badminton – with more undulating terrain and a tight fifteen-minute time limit."

Avery looked out the window of the truck. "And certainly there is no more beautiful place in all of Britain to ride," he said. "Although, when you're bent down at a flat gallop against the clock and coming in to attack an enormous rough-sawn elephant trap I very much doubt you'll be taking time to look at the scenic wonders!"

Avery was right. All the same, as Issie took her first glimpse of the estate on her cross-country course walk that Wednesday evening, she marvelled at the beauty of the place, the pretty groves of trees and the wonderful swards of green pasture that she would be galloping along in just a few days' time. Right now the fields were still being grazed by sheep, but on Saturday morning there would be thousands of spectators here, standing behind the rope barriers and watching the great and the good as they tackled the cross-country course.

Even with Kentucky and Badminton under her belt, Issie was still in total awe of the list of competitors that she would be up against. The names were all so familiar to her – many of them had been her heroes ever since she was a pony-club kid. There was the incredible Oliver Townend, who had risen from humble Huddersfield beginnings to conquer the eventing world. There was Andrew Nicholson, a New Zealander whose ability to stay onboard a horse no matter what had earnt him the nickname 'Mr Stickability'. There was the immeasurably posh William Fox-Pitt, who rode his horses with a feline grace, the rock-solid Mary King who always kept her horse in perfect control and the feisty, super-talented Polly Stockton who charged fences fearlessly and had the nine lives of a cat.

Naturally, when she saw the photographers crowding

around a rider at the media tent on the Thursday morning before the trotting-up, Issie assumed it was for one of the many mega-stars competing. Then she caught a glimpse of the pouting blonde in purple jodhpurs striking a pose for the cameras with a moon-faced thug sulking alongside her.

Yes, Natasha Tucker was here at Burghley! Despite the fact that she wasn't even riding, and that her last two competitions had ended in elimination, the paparazzi still followed her every move!

"I don't understand it!" Kate shook her head in disbelief. "There's all these famous riders here, why do they want a photograph of Stuck-up Tucker? She's not even riding! And who is that posing with her? I don't recognise him."

"He's not a rider, he's a footballer," Stella groaned. "That's Lance Emmanuel."

In a way, Issie was relieved that the media storm was focused on the 'famous' Natasha Tucker. Issie was already under so much pressure that the last thing she needed was more attention and...

"Issie!" Natasha Tucker waved at her across the room and raced over to join her with the photographers following in her wake and Lance Emmanuel looking sullen and out of place as he walked behind her.

Natasha flung herself at Issie and gave her an over-the-top air-kiss on both cheeks as the photographers started snapping wildly.

"I was just telling these lovely media gentlemen that there's no longer a rivalry between us," Natasha smiled.

"There isn't?" Issie was bewildered. "Was there ever one?"

"Oh, Issie!" Natasha shrieked with fake laughter. "You're so funny. Anyway, I was telling the boys that you and I are actually such good friends that you've offered to model a pair of my new Natty T jodhpurs today when you lead your horses in the trotting-up."

Issie had already chosen her trotting-up outfit– a pair of plain cream jods and a chic black shirt. Now, with the barrels of a dozen cameras trained on her, she felt herself turning queasy at the sight of Natasha's latest addition to her clothing line – a pair of bright purple jods with a floral pattern on the sticky bum and the giant initials N and T smack in the middle of the rider's backside.

Natasha leaned in close as she offered Issie the jodhpurs. "Go on, Issie, be a sport," she muttered. "I need to sell these hideous things somehow. Do this for me? Please don't cause a scene…"

Issie stood back for a moment and took in the full spectacle that was Natasha. Yes, there was the fake tan, the hair extensions and the lurid purple clothes, but beneath that she saw a glimpse of something more. This was the same Natasha Tucker she'd gone to pony club with — the miserable girl with no mates and a pushy mum who had forced her daughter to ride and paid for posh ponies that Natasha didn't even want. The same girl whose father only paid her attention when he thought he could turn a quick buck out of his own child, by selling the pony club out from underneath her.

Beneath the sassy, trashy society girl image, there was a heart. Issie knew that Natasha had been devastated when her parents divorced. All she'd ever really wanted was love and approval, and look what she'd ended up with. A lout of a boyfriend and paparazzi idiots snapping her every move…

Issie sighed and took the jods from Natasha's hands.

"Where's the changing room?"

And so, as the procession of world-famous riders and their equally starry horses lined up to take their trot in front of the judges on the forecourt of palatial Burghley House, Issie Brown took her place alongside them wearing bright purple breeches with Natasha Tucker's initials on her butt.

There was a loud wolf whistle and Issie turned around to see a grinning Marcus Pearce coming towards her leading Velluto Rosso.

"What's with the purple pants?" Marcus frowned.

"Don't ask," Issie groaned. "I'm doing a favour for a friend. Well, a favour for an enemy, really… it's complicated."

"OK," Marcus said, "but if you turn up for the dressage tomorrow in a pink bunny costume then I'm going to have to step in and stop you, OK?"

"It's a deal," Issie said.

"Marcus Pearce? You're next." The trotting-up steward beckoned for Marcus to come up to the tarmac strip.

"I better go," Marcus said. "Stop distracting me when I'm trying to compete!"

"Very funny," Issie smiled back. "Good luck."

Issie watched him leave and realised just how much she had been looking forward to running into him here at Burghley. Marcus somehow made her heart flutter in the same way that approaching the Vicarage Ditch at Badminton did.

She wished she had been wearing something a little more flattering for her reunion with him. How did she manage to let Natasha talk her into doing this? The Natty T purple and floral jods reached a whole new height of hideousness – and there was a definite titter from the crowd as Issie came out to run her two horses for the judges.

Both of them passed the trot-up with flying colours. "I think those jods might be the best ruse yet," Avery told her afterwards. "The judges were so blinded by their purpleness your horse could have been running on three legs and they still wouldn't have noticed."

Issie was just relieved that the trotting-up was done. The horses were ready and so was she. Tomorrow morning the Burghley Horse Trials began – and she was in the dressage arena at 10 a.m.

CHAPTER 11

Issie's hands were trembling at her throat as she tried to tie her cravat the next morning. She stood in the tiny, cramped bathroom of the horse truck, peering into the mirror as she fumbled with the fabric and her silver tie pin. When the pin slipped, she stabbed her own finger and let out a yelp, then paused and took a deep breath and exhaled, and then another and another, trying to calm down. She had to regain her composure! Horses could sense even the slightest bit of tension in their rider – and Nightstorm was super-sensitive. Issie had to force herself to relax and keep her head.

Taking more calming deep breaths she waited until her hands were steady and then finished tying up the cravat. She was sitting on the banquette zipping up her long black boots when the horse-truck door opened. It was Avery.

"I just wanted to let you know you've got exactly fifteen minutes before you are due to perform," he told her. "That doesn't give you much time."

"I don't need much time," Issie said.

Avery nodded in agreement. "We'll do it just like you planned. I'll tell Stella to bring Storm around to the arena. We'll meet you there."

Normally, Issie would have been down at the arena an hour ago, riding to prepare Nightstorm before the competition. But today Issie was about to try something that she had never done before. She was about to ride Storm straight into the main arena completely cold. She was doing the dressage test with absolutely no warm-up.

"No warm-up?" Stella had looked aghast when Issie first told her the idea. "But that's crazy! I've never heard of anyone riding a test without working their horse in first. You'll go into the arena and fall apart!"

Issie shook her head. "Stella, don't you see? Storm is always fine during his warm-up phase. And then after fifteen minutes he begins to act up. But what if there was no warm-up phase? If we went straight into the arena to begin our test then he wouldn't have the chance to get bored!"

Stella thought about this logic for a moment. "OK, but you're not going to get the chance to test the theory in competition until you're actually in the arena at Burghley."

"I know," Issie said. "That's the risk I'm going to have to take."

As Avery shut the truck door behind him, Issie turned back to the mirror once more. She tucked a hairnet over the top of her sleek chignon, then she took her tailcoat out of the dry-cleaning bag hanging on the door of the truck. She slipped it on carefully, her hands steady now as she did up the gold buttons. She reached for the top hat that was sitting on the table and pushed it down firmly onto her head, and then pulled on the white leather dressage gloves that completed her outfit. She was ready. She only hoped Nightstorm was too.

Stella and Avery were waiting for her at the arena gates, with Nightstorm completely tacked up, when she arrived.

"How is he?" Issie asked Stella.

"He's in a good mood," Stella said. "He was nickering to me at the stable door when I arrived this morning to groom him. He's totally chilled out."

"Good," Issie said.

Avery looked at his watch. "The competitor in the ring is just about to finish their test," he said. "You'll be on in two minutes."

"Right," Issie said. "You better leg me up then."

Avery gave Issie a boost into the saddle while Stella held the reins to keep Nightstorm still.

Once Issie was onboard, Stella tightened the girth a final hole and then the head groom and trainer both stood back and left her to ride alone in through the wings of the stadium and into the main arena.

As Issie entered the grandstand, she could hear the applause from the crowd for the previous competitor now leaving the dressage arena. Issie looked around at the packed stadium as Mike Partridge's voice broke the silence over the loudspeaker.

"Our next rider, Isadora Brown, has just taken out the honours at both the Kentucky and the Badminton Horse Trials," Mike Partridge announced.

"Here at Burghley, she's riding two horses and the first of these is this stunning bay stallion. Isadora told me at the riders' briefing that she's had trouble in the past controlling Nightstorm in the dressage arena. However, she's confident that his problems are solved now just in time for Burghley..."

Issie shortened up her reins and urged Storm into a trot. "This better work," she muttered under her breath to the bay stallion, "or I'm going to look pretty stupid when you buck me off in the middle of the arena."

It was the moment of truth. This was a gamble and Issie knew it. Without a warm-up session her only preparation was a few laps of the outside of the dressage barrier to get Storm on the bit and listening to her before she entered the arena to start her test.

The shrill tone of the bell sounded and she gathered Storm up beneath her and rode one last lap outside, pushing the stallion into an extended trot, then turning him at a canter to enter at A and carry on down the centre line. As she rode the line, her adrenalin was surging. They were now in the arena and all eyes were on them!

The first halt was square. Storm stood like a statue waiting for his next cue. They needed to execute a working trot straight away and as Issie put her legs on she felt the horse rise up underneath her, his hindquarters engaging and powering him forward. She knew at that moment that she was in for a perfect ride. For the next three and half minutes, as they rode half-passes and counter-canters, loops and serpentines, Storm was at his most brilliant. The stallion seemed to float above the ground, his hooves barely touching the sand of the arena as he performed faultlessly. Issie only had to think of a movement and it would happen. It was as if Storm could read her mind, as he effortlessly changed pace or shifted tempo, extending his trot, then pulling back and reacting precisely at the next marker. As they came down the centre line to do their flying changes, Issie could have sworn that the stallion's canter strides were keeping pace with her own heartbeat as they danced their way through a performance that would have put the El Caballo stallions to shame.

On the loudspeaker, Mike Partridge was beside himself with delight at the performance.

"This is *haute école* quality stuff from this young combination," Mike Partridge raved. "There is no question that this difficult stallion is doing the best test of his career in the arena today. And now they finish by coming back up the centre line to salute the judges…"

The spectators had been hushed and reverent all this time as Issie rode her test, but once she had saluted and it was finally over an enormous cheer rose from the crowds in the grandstands. Issie had ridden it exquisitely. As she came out of the main arena, she vaulted down off Storm's back and threw her arms around her horse. The no-warm-up technique had worked! Storm had just delivered the perfect dressage test.

Even before they heard the score, Avery and Stella were whooping with delight and congratulating Issie. When the scores were finally posted and Issie got an incredible 37, Stella's shrieks could be heard all the way across the other side of the arena.

There was more excitement to come when Issie entered the arena again for the second time that day on Victory.

Unlike the temperamental Storm, Victory required a decent warm-up and Issie spent over half an hour working the brown gelding in before she took him into the arena. It was a faultless performance. Victory was a total schoolmaster and he never missed a beat. With his Thoroughbred blood, Victory lacked the presence and charisma of Storm who had stunned the crowd with his striking, elevated paces. All the same, he scored an excellent 39 that put him into fifth place on the leaderboard.

Storm's score of 37 proved to be unbeatable and by the end of the day, Issie was gobsmacked when she realised that they were in first place after the dressage!

That evening back at the horse truck, the team ate dinner and talked their way through any issues that might arise on the cross-country course the next day.

"The ground is wetter than I expected with all the rain they had last week," Avery said. "I think we should use the big studs in their hind shoes."

Stella nodded. "I've already laid them out ready to fit

in the morning. And I'll be sure to put loads of grease on their front and back legs to help them slide over any fences in case they catch themselves on a jump."

"We'll put tendon boots on front and back legs as well, obviously," Kate added. "They'll be well protected from any scrapes or cuts."

Avery pulled out the call sheet for the morning. "I've double-checked your start times," he said. "You're on Victory first at eleven-fifteen. You ride Nightstorm second – and you're up on him at two-thirty in the starters' box."

Issie sat at the table, pushing her dinner around on the plate without actually eating it. She was too sick with excitement to touch the food. Tomorrow was the most dangerous and thrilling phase of the three-day event and she had butterflies doing loop-the-loops in her belly right now.

She sat and listened to Avery running through his usual checklist, as if this was just another competition. But everyone sitting at the table knew that it was much more than that. This was the biggest test of her career. With each phase Issie came one step closer to the Burghley trophy, one step nearer to achieving her incredible goal of the Grand Slam.

If Issie actually let herself think about how vital her performance was tomorrow then she would fall apart with nerves. So, instead of dwelling on it, she did the only vaguely useful thing she could think of doing. She went down to the stables to check on the horses.

Considering her bad luck at Badminton, she wouldn't have been at all surprised to arrive and find one of them about to go down with a bout of colic. She was relieved to see that both her horses were standing happily in their boxes.

Issie let herself into Storm's loose box and bolted the door behind her. Then she dug about in the grooming kit and took out a stiff-bristled brush to work on his legs. Running the brush down his hindquarters, she checked out the scars on his left hock. The stallion had recovered completely from his injury and Francoise was confident that the fitness training they'd done had him back in peak condition. In fact, the Frenchwoman insisted he was in even better shape than he had been before.

Issie rummaged in the grooming kit again and took out a soft-bristled brush this time, working it over the stallion's face, making sure she got his favourite spot right behind the ears where the bridle sat. Storm lowered his head contentedly and shut his eyes. "Good boy," Issie said, "that's right. You get some sleep. You've got a big day tomorrow."

She left Storm and moved on to the next stall, refilling Victory's hay net which was almost empty. The brown gelding was moving about restlessly in his box. He was an experienced competitor and he knew that the cross-country was looming. Issie tied the hay net off to the ring on the wall and then as Victory stepped forward to take a pick of the hay she ran her hands over his body, tracing her fingers across the muscles of his shoulder. He looked so much stronger and fitter than he had done when he arrived at The Laurels a month ago, but was he fit enough to handle the demanding countryside he'd be galloping across tomorrow? Issie knew that Victory had the heart and the courage – she had her fingers crossed he had the stamina too.

Issie had refilled the water troughs in both stalls and was just about to leave, when she felt a chill run through her. She turned around, half expecting to see the familiar grey shape of a pony, a pair of coal-black eyes staring at her.

"Mystic?" she called out. Then she heard the soft pad

of footsteps in the corridor and the Burghley Stables night guard was standing there with a torch, shining it on her.

"Everything OK in here, miss?" the guard asked.

"Uh-huh," Issie said. "I'm fine."

Walking out into the stable yard, Issie's eyes searched the blackness, but if Mystic had been there a moment ago, he was gone now.

Years later, when she reflected on this moment, she would wonder whether the grey pony had actually been there. She had certainly sensed something. But the guard had interrupted them at that crucial moment, fate had intervened and she saw nothing in the darkness. And so she left the stables and went to bed, aiming to get a decent night's sleep, ready to face the cross-country in the morning.

Cross-country began at nine-thirty on the dot and by the time Issie and Victory were preparing to enter the start box there had already been nine riders go around the course. None of them so far had delivered a clear round.

"The track is riding incredibly tight against the clock," Avery told her as he legged her up onto Victory. "The only two clear rounds so far have racked up time faults on their scores."

Issie had known from the start that this course would need to be ridden fast if she wanted to hit the minute markers. But Avery was right – even the quick riders had been found out on this track. She would have to put a bomb under Victory if they were going to make the time.

Kate did a last-minute gear check and then Avery led Issie and Victory forward to the box. Victory loved the cross-country phase and he was so keen that Issie had to restrain him, gripping the reins as the gelding danced about while the steward faffed with his paperwork.

Finally, the steward was ready and he lined them up as the timer was cued. "On your marks, get set, and... go!"

Victory broke from the start box like a racehorse and Issie leaned forward, her eyes already focused straight ahead on the very first jump.

The hayfeeder was one of those uncomplicated fences, perfect for getting a horse into a stride, and Victory flew it without a second thought and powered on in a beautiful gallop to fence two, the flowerbed.

The gelding took it brilliantly and Issie's confidence surged as she pressed her horse on, his strides swallowing up the ground. They would have to be swift around this course – that meant taking the fences fast and taking risks.

At the picnic table Victory flew the massive spread without even slowing down, galloping down the long, green sward ahead, and it wasn't until they were a few strides out from the staircase that Issie hit the brakes. Always the perfect schoolmaster, Victory slowed down on cue so that he was almost trotting as they took the two giant leaps down the bank. Then he changed gear and went back into a gallop, taking a beautiful forward stride into the trakehner.

In the announcer's box, Mike Partridge had been joined for the cross-country phase by former world champion eventer Jilly Jones, as Issie came into fence number six.

"They've nicknamed this sequence of jumps Natasha's Purple Pimples," Jilly was telling the crowd. "The wooden fences are sponsored by Natty T equestrian clothing – the pimple shape, as you can see, is really round and very narrow for the horses to jump – but look at the classy way this big brown gelding handles himself, taking the two elements with ease and galloping on now towards the dog leg."

"He's got a lovely gallop on him," Mike Partridge took over, "an Australian Thoroughbred, owned originally by Mrs Tulia Disbrowe who sold him recently to a syndicate. He was briefly ridden by Natasha Tucker but now the syndicate have given the ride back to Issie Brown and they are no doubt anxious to see him finish at the top of the leaderboard today – and who better to get him there than this young lady? She's heading into the lake now, and to ride this lake you need maximum control. The horses need to pop down a very steep drop over a brush into the water and then through the water and back out again onto the bank and then just one stride to a second brush at a harsh angle and back around into the water to jump one last element and then an easy canter out of the pond. And look at this! Isadora and Victory have just managed it beautifully!"

Out on the course, Issie could feel that Victory was

at full gallop, but as they headed towards the Elephant Trap she put her legs on and asked for even more. They had just passed a minute marker and were barely keeping up with the clock. They had to keep going at full throttle if they were going to make the punishing time.

The Elephant Trap was a massive jump and a real 'rider frightener', totally treacherous in appearance. But Issie's blood was up and she was riding with such determination that she barely gave it a glance before Victory popped the rough-sawn wooden fence.

She was less cavalier about the Cheddar Corner, where the jumps were tight triangle wedges set at strange angles on top of tricky, undulating terrain that required killer precision to make it through without a run-out.

She manoeuvred Victory deftly through the cheddar wedges and then, straight after the corners, came a massive log jump that led down a steep bank to a road, and then back up the hill to another rustic corner at a very complex angle.

Victory showed exactly how clever he was at this last corner, negotiating the dips and twists in the turf and taking the jump on a perfect forward stride. Issie put her legs on again straight away, but this time, she didn't feel the response that she'd been hoping for. Victory was flagging! They were less than halfway around this massive course and if her horse was tiring already, they would never make it in under the time!

As they cleared the next jump, a straightforward hedge, Issie tried once more to push Victory on to gallop harder. When the brown gelding failed to respond she made the decision not to push him. She let him gallop at his own speed, and waited to check his progress at the next minute marker. When she clocked her speed on the stopwatch she saw that they had slipped back by a massive six seconds since the last marker!

Trying not to panic about the time, Issie realised that if Victory was tired then the most important thing was to get him to the finish line. Time penalties seemed unavoidable now. The main thing was to conserve energy so that her horse had enough gas in the tank to make it home.

Some of the biggest jumps on the course were still to come – and the next fence, the Centaur's Leap, would be a real test.

Of all the fences this was the one with the reputation

for eliminating more combinations than any other. The massive Centaur's Leap had the same mind-boggling dimensions as the Gamekeeper's Brush at Kentucky. A deep chasm of a ditch prefaced a hedge that stood almost three metres back from the take-off point. The horses would have to get up a huge head of steam and all their courage to launch themselves from the groundline at the start of the ditch and then fly the hedge without stumbling.

As they galloped in to the Centaur's Leap Issie knew that the gelding was losing speed, but she was sure that he was scopey and experienced enough to make it over this jump. But when she was five strides out she suddenly realised they were coming in on a mis-stride just like they had done in Kentucky!

Issie didn't panic. Instead, she kicked on and growled at Victory and the gelding did exactly what he had been trained to do. He pushed himself forward, took four big strides and then launched himself into the air like a superstar, taking the Centaur's Leap on a perfect forward stride.

On the other side of the fence, Issie gave the big brown gelding a slappy pat on his neck. Victory was frothy with sweat, his breathing coming hard and raspy. The last fence had really taken it out of him. Issie was no longer looking at the watch on her wrist. Her only concern was getting him home.

The next fence on the course was The Grove. Shaded beneath a spreading canopy of large trees, this fence was deceptive because the horses came in blind, unable to see the jumps hidden in the shadows until they were almost on top of them.

The first jump in the sequence was a massive hedge, then there was a single stride to a big drop and then another stride before the horses had to pop another downhill hedge where the landing fell away sharply on the other side, completing the series. The three jumps required absolute precision as jumping downhill was a dangerous business.

Coming into the first element, Issie slowed Victory down so that he could take a good look at the fence and then urged the gelding with her legs to pop the hedge neatly and put in a good stride before heading down the bank. Victory was really exhausted now, and instead of gathering up his energy in the stride between the bank and the next hedge, he seemed to slump. Issie had to virtually pick him up with her hands to encourage him over the last element. She felt Victory rise up underneath her, but he was too slow as he tucked up his front legs and suddenly they were in big trouble.

Victory's left foreleg managed to get left behind, caught on the top rail of the hedge. With one leg wrenched backwards, the horse jack-knifed through the air, turning a complete somersault with Issie still on his back.

As he came crashing down on the other side of the jump Issie knew she could be crushed beneath him so she thrust herself free of the saddle and out of the horse's trajectory. She landed to the side of the hedge on her belly and heard the pop and hiss as her airtech jacket inflated to protect her as she skidded on the wet grass. The jacket absorbed most of the shock of the fall and apart from grass-stained knees and ripped riding gloves she was unharmed. Issie stumbled to her feet and looked for her horse. Victory was a few metres away from her, next to the hedge where he had fallen. He was utterly exhausted, his sides heaving in and out like bellows, his whole body wet and foamy with sweat. Issie raced forward to grab him by the reins and lead him out of the path of the fence and that was when she saw that he was holding his front leg aloft. It was the leg that he had hooked on the fence, and Issie realised that it must have been twisted terribly, stuck behind him as he somersaulted.

She tried to coax the horse to step forward so she could see just how bad the damage was. Victory was holding the leg completely off the ground, unwilling to put it down. She looked at the leg more closely. The point of the elbow was sticking out at a strange angle. Issie's blood ran cold. Victory's leg was broken.

CHAPTER 12

On the sidelines, the crowd who had seen Victory fall had no idea just how serious this really was. But Issie's face was ashen, her voice broken with emotion as she shouted out to the jump steward who was running towards her. "Get the vet! Now!"

Victory was trembling and heaving but mercifully the gelding had the common sense to stay still. Issie moved to the horse's side and reached out to examine the leg. Victory flinched and she took her hand away as she didn't want to upset him, but that brief touch had told her all that she needed to know. She had felt the bone sticking out beneath the skin. The leg was definitely broken. She was certain. And with that certainty came the awful realisation that this was the end.

This wonderful talented horse who had never given her anything less than his best, who had been her partner all the way around this difficult and exhausting cross-country course and so many courses before this one, had paid the ultimate price for his honesty and courage. "Ohmygod, Victory." Issie stroked the horse's muzzle. "I'm so sorry. I'm so sorry. I'm so sorry…"

All Issie could do was to cradle his muzzle in her arms and whisper her anguish as she stood there helplessly waiting for the vet.

It seemed like forever, but it must have been only a few minutes before the emergency vet arrived. He examined the leg and confirmed the diagnosis.

"It's broken at the elbow," he said solemnly.

Issie looked into Victory's deep brown eyes. His face was so noble and beautiful despite the pain he must have been in. He stood calmly beside her because he trusted her – and she was about to betray that trust in the most awful way imaginable – but what else could she do? She couldn't bear the thought of what was about to happen, but she didn't want this magnificent horse to suffer. She nodded her permission to the vet.

"I'll go and get the screens then," he said.

Issie had never seen a horse put down but she knew what the vet meant. The screens were foldaway hospital blinds that vets carried at events like this one and used to erect around the horse so that the animal could be kept private from the crowds when the lethal injection was given.

As Issie watched the vet walk off to his van, hot tears ran down her cheeks. She hugged Victory tight to her chest, trying desperately to be brave for her horse. It was the most awful moment – and it was all being played out in front of thousands of spectators still crowding the sidelines, looking at the injured horse and the rider in floods of tears beside him.

"Issie!" There was a cry from behind the crowd barriers as Kate Knight pushed her way through the throng of spectators. A steward tried to stop her but Issie shouted him down. "Let her through! She's my groom!"

Kate ran down the steep bank, red-faced and panting as she reached Issie's side.

"I was back at the truck getting the cool-down kit

ready when I heard the news," she managed to gasp. "I ran all the way…"

Kate looked at the tears streaming down Issie's cheeks. "Issie? What is it? What did the vet say?"

"It's broken," Issie said. "They've just gone to get the screens."

"Ohmygod!" Kate was shocked. "Issie, no! Are you sure?"

Issie nodded. "I could feel the bone sticking out through the skin."

"Which bone?" Kate asked, stepping forward closer to the horse. "Do you mind if I take a look at him?"

Issie shook her head silently and Kate began to examine Victory. She was still bent over looking at the leg when the vet returned.

"We'll just take a minute to set the screens up," he told Issie gently. "He won't have to suffer for much longer…"

"No," Kate said. "Don't set them up." The vet frowned at her. "Who are you?"

"I'm Victory's groom," Kate said. "And I'm also training to be a vet. I don't think this horse needs to be put down."

The vet took a deep breath. "I don't know what school you're attending, young lady, but it's pretty clear this horse has a broken leg…"

"…at the apex of the elbow," Kate finished his sentence. "I believe a horse with a very similar injury was recently operated on at the veterinary research institute in Glasgow and enjoyed a full recovery."

The vet looked taken aback. "That was experimental surgery," he said, "the technology is still in its early stages…"

"But it worked, didn't it?" Kate replied. "The colt lived. We studied the case at vet school. So if it's worked for one horse, then it can work for another. They can try the same procedure on Victory."

The vet looked at the anxious faces of the two young women in front of him and realised that he needed to answer this question very carefully. "It would be a long and risky procedure. It would cost a fortune and you might not get the result you want. This horse will probably never compete again."

"But he would live?" Issie clarified. "If you took him to Glasgow and they did this operation?"

The vet sighed. "It's possible."

"Then you're not putting up those screens," Issie told him through gritted teeth. "Go and get a horse box now. I don't care if he never competes again. If we have any chance at all of saving his life then please do whatever it takes."

The next fifteen minutes became a flurry of activity on the cross-country course. The stewards had radioed back to the start line and all other riders had been stopped. Issie, who had been in the same position at Badminton, knew that the riders would be stressed out by the wait and she felt pressure to hurry so that the competition could resume. If Victory wouldn't be loaded into the box then she knew she would be forced to reconsider her decision.

Luckily Victory seemed to realise that Issie and Kate were trying to help him and when the emergency horse box was towed onto the field the brown gelding didn't resist. He managed to limp into it on three legs and stood willingly as the girls locked him in.

Issie stayed in the box with him for the journey back, feeling anxious about every bump as the Range Rover slowly, carefully towed the horse box back to the stables. Meanwhile, Kate was in the front seat on her mobile phone talking to the team at the Glasgow Institute. By the time they were back at the stables and Avery had joined them Kate had it all arranged.

"They say they'll need to look at him to assess whether he's a candidate for the surgery," Kate said. "I have to take him there as soon as possible."

"Did the surgeons tell you what his chances are?" Avery asked bluntly. "What are the odds that he'll make it through this?"

Kate shook her head. "They sounded positive when I spoke to them but they emphasised that they've only done this procedure once before…"

Avery looked serious. "Victory's in a lot of pain right now, Kate. If this isn't going to work…"

"If I truly thought that he had no chance then I'd say fine, put him out of his misery," Kate agreed, "but these guys in Glasgow are the best, Tom. At least this gives him a fighting chance."

"Getting him all the way from here to Glasgow is going to be a mission," Avery said.

Kate nodded, "We'll need to create a special travelling box inside the horse truck with a support sling to take Victory's weight off the injured leg for the journey. And we'll need to do it quick. It's a four-hour drive to Glasgow – maybe five hours if we take it slow to protect the leg. If we can get him there tonight in good shape then they may operate first thing tomorrow."

Avery considered what Kate was telling him and then he pulled out his mobile phone. "I'll get one of the Burghley carpenters who repair the cross-country jumps to secure a partition in the truck and then we can pad it so Victory is comfortable. The sling should be easy, there's a hook that we can attach to the roof…"

Issie was flooded with relief. Avery was in agreement with Kate. They were going to do this!

She turned to Kate. "What can I do?"

"Pack Victory's bags," Kate told her. "Get his rugs and his hard feed, fill the hay nets and make sure he's got enough water for the journey."

Issie was only too pleased to be assigned duties. They took her mind off the awfulness of what had just happened. Incredibly, by the time she had assembled everything Victory needed Avery had built a divider panel with padding in the horse truck, with a sling attached to the ceiling, and had hired a driver for the trip. The three of them then gently coaxed Victory onboard.

"The vet has given him a sedative to ease the pain; it should last the whole journey. I'll travel in the back with him and make sure he's OK," Kate reassured Issie as they attached the sling belt around Victory's belly and hoisted him up in the harness.

"And you'll call us as soon as you get there?" Issie asked.

"Absolutely," Kate confirmed. She stepped into the loose box and Avery bolted it shut with her inside. Then she waved them goodbye as they shut the ramp, closing her into the back of the truck along with Victory.

Issie and Avery stood and watched as the driver started the engine and slowly eased the truck towards the security gates.

"What if he doesn't cope with the journey to Glasgow?" Issie's lips were trembling as she fought back the tears.

"He'll make it," Avery replied. "Issie, his chances are good. Kate is with him and the Glasgow team are pioneers in this field—"

Avery suddenly stopped speaking. The horse truck seemed to be stalled at the gates. The driver had been stopped at the security barrier and now he was getting out of the truck cab.

"What the blue blazes is going on up there?" Avery said. "Why has the guard stopped them?"

The security guard and the truck driver were now engrossed in conversation, and a third man standing with the guard caught Issie's attention. He was wearing a dark grey suit and appeared to be issuing directions to the truck driver.

"Oh no, oh no, oh NO!" Issie broke into a run, headed for the truck. They were in trouble – Victory was in trouble. The man at the gates was Oliver Tucker.

Oliver Tucker already had the ramp of the truck lowered and was shouting orders by the time Issie and Avery got there.

"You listen to me!" Oliver Tucker was fuming. "That horse is my property and I am demanding that you take him off right now!"

"Over my dead body!" Kate shot back.

"It's not you that I'm interested in!" Oliver Tucker replied. "It's his dead body that I want!"

"Oliver!" Avery ran up the ramp to intervene. "What

do you think you're doing? Do you want to tell me what on earth is going on?"

"You've got a cheek!" Oliver Tucker rounded on him. "You can't remove this horse without my permission. I own him!"

"You mean the syndicate owns him!" Issie clarified.

Oliver Tucker shot her a filthy glare. "Whatever!" he snarled. "My point is that you don't just ship a horse off for expensive medical treatment without getting the permission of the owners beforehand."

"We didn't think we needed anyone's permission to save his life!" Kate replied.

"Well, you do!" Oliver Tucker said coldly. "This truck ride alone is going to cost a fortune. Vets' bills at this fancy place you're taking him to will be exorbitant!"

Issie tried to stay calm. She had to give Oliver Tucker the benefit of the doubt. Maybe he didn't understand what they were doing here.

"The Glasgow Institute have state-of-the-art facilities. There's a chance that they can fix the broken leg. Victory won't have to be put down."

Oliver Tucker looked at her as if she were as thick as a plank.

"And what would be the point of that?" he harrumphed.

"We could save his life," Issie said.

"I've spoken to the vet who examined him," Oliver Tucker said. "He said he advised putting him down on the spot and you refused. He says the horse will never compete again – even if he does recover he'll be ruined as an eventer. And he's a gelding so he's useless for breeding. All it amounts to is a total waste of money!"

Issie was incredulous, "Saving his life is hardly worthless!"

"That's up to the syndicate to decide," Oliver Tucker snapped. "And since I run the syndicate, I say that he's being put down here and now. Get him off the truck."

"Oliver," Avery stepped in, "the horse is staying on the truck. Time is vital here. The most important thing is to let the surgeons in Glasgow save his life."

"The most important thing is my money!" Oliver Tucker retorted. "And I can tell you that you won't be seeing a penny of it. You can't possibly expect my syndicate to pay through the nose for an accident caused by your jockey."

"What?!" Avery frowned.

"Her!" Tucker pointed an accusatory finger at Issie. "She's the one who got us into this mess with her sloppy riding. She did this to the horse! It's her fault."

"Issie did nothing wrong," Avery shot back. "She rode that fence perfectly. The reason the horse went down at that jump was because he was tired – and that's because his fitness regime fell apart while he was in your hands for the past three months. You want to talk about who was to blame for this? Take a look in the mirror! Or maybe talk to your syndicate who care more about money than horses. But don't you dare start to throw muck at my rider!"

Issie didn't say anything. She was so horrified at the accusation she couldn't speak.

"She rode him to his death," Oliver Tucker insisted. "Now she's too cowardly to deliver the final blow and put the beast out of his misery. Well, I'm not! I'll do it for her!"

He turned to the security guard. "Help me get the horse off the truck! I'll shoot him myself if I have to!"

With the guard beside him, Oliver Tucker stormed up the ramp and began to unbolt the loose box.

Avery rushed forward to stop him, but the security guard stepped in and held him back. Watching the disaster unfolding in front of her, Issie had never felt more powerless in her life.

Victory was going to die – and there wasn't a thing she could do to stop it.

CHAPTER 13

Oliver Tucker unbuckled the sling and took hold of Victory's lead rope.

"Come on!" he shouted at the brown gelding, "Move it!"

"Leave him alone!" Kate shouted. "If you move him it could hurt his leg."

"As if I care!" Oliver Tucker said. He began to haul on the rope, trying to force Victory to step out on his broken leg and down the ramp.

"Don't do this, Oliver!" Avery warned him.

"Shut up!" Oliver Tucker said, grunting as he pulled at the rope. Victory wasn't moving. Oliver Tucker let go of the rope and seized a whip from the corner of the truck and waved it at the horse. "This will get him going…"

"NO!"

The cry didn't come from Issie, Avery or Kate.

It came from a blonde girl in purple jodhpurs standing on the ramp of the truck and looking on aghast at the man about to beat a horse with a broken leg.

"Dad? What's going on here?"

"Natasha!" Oliver Tucker lowered the whip hastily. "I'm trying to do what's best for the poor horse…"

Issie cut him off. "Victory has a broken leg. We want to take him to Glasgow so they can operate. Your dad wants to shoot him."

Natasha Tucker's face fell. "Dad? Is that true?"

Oliver Tucker looked shamefaced. "I'm just being practical, darling…"

"Right," Natasha said darkly. "Just like you were being practical when you took him off me and gave him to Issie to ride?"

Avery and Issie had been trying to appeal to Oliver Tucker's decency and kindness – which was pointless since he didn't have any. But Natasha knew exactly how to deal with her father.

"Think, Dad!" she snapped. "If you take this horse off the truck and put him down it's going to totally destroy the Natty T brand."

"I don't see how it's anybody's business!" Oliver Tucker railed. "It's my horse and my money…"

"…and my reputation!" Natasha shot back. "No one will buy my jodhpurs if word gets out that my family are a bunch of horse killers! How is that going to look on the front page of the Daily Mail?"

"That's right!" Issie leapt in, backing Natasha up. "We'll tell the papers that you had the chance to save the horse and you refused."

Oliver Tucker hesitated. Then he let go of Victory's leadrope in disgust. "All right! Take the stupid beast to the vet!" he snapped at Avery as he pushed past him. "And good luck to you!"

There was silence as they watched Oliver Tucker stomp off down the ramp and out of the yard. His dramatic departure was slightly ruined when he trod in horse dung and swore blue murder as he tried unsuccessfully to scrape it off his shoe as he stormed away.

Avery and Kate went to take care of Victory and Issie

turned to Natasha. "Thanks," she said. "I know it must have been tough, standing up to your dad like that…"

"I didn't do it for you," Natasha said flatly. "I know what you think of me. I know you don't respect me as a rider, and I know you find it hard to believe that I care about Victory. But I do. Maybe I am talentless, but I'm not heartless. He was my horse too you know."

Natasha turned her back on Issie and began to walk away. Then she turned back again and looked Issie straight in the eye. "You have to let me know if he's OK. As soon as you have news from Glasgow?"

Issie nodded. "I will. I promise."

The sling was reattached and Victory was settled back in his travel box again with Kate. Issie and Tom stood and watched as the truck departed the gates, without incident this time.

"Come on," Avery said. "You've done everything you can for him. Let's get back to the stables and see how

Stella is doing with Nightstorm."

Nightstorm! Through all the drama of the past few hours Issie hadn't given a single thought to her second ride. Victory had been all that had mattered. But now she saw her instructor's expectant face, and she knew what Avery was thinking.

"Tom," she shook her head. "No. I can't! I can't ride that course again."

"Issie," Avery said, "I know what you've just been through was terrible, but you're sitting in first place on Nightstorm. You could win Burghley. You're in line to win the Grand Slam."

"No," Issie shook her head again. "I'm not doing it, Tom. I can't." She suddenly felt like she couldn't breathe as she struggled to get the words out.

"Issie, you can't let this set-back ruin your chances." Avery was adamant. "You've got to get back on the horse."

"Even if it kills him?" Issie said. She looked down at her feet, and the words came out in a whisper. "Tom, what if Oliver Tucker was right? What if the crash was my fault?"

Avery was surprised. "Oliver Tucker was trying to be

cruel. You rode that jump perfectly – it wasn't your fault."

"But it was!" Issie gasped. "I knew Victory was tired, Tom! I knew he wasn't coping but I kept going. I should have stopped him. I should have withdrawn when he started to slow up. He was never going to make it around that course…"

"Issie, you mustn't do this to yourself, you're emotionally exhausted. You need to rest before you ride this afternoon…"

"I'm not riding today – or ever again!" Issie shot back. "It's over!" And with that, she turned and ran towards the stables.

In floods of tears, Issie rounded the corner of Storm's loose box. She slid the door open and then shut it again behind her and collapsed down into the straw on the floor at Storm's feet, sobbing her heart out.

She knew that Avery was probably furious with her right now, and she wished she could explain to her instructor properly. How could she take Storm out on that same course and live through it all again? She loved the bay stallion so much, she couldn't bear to risk losing him…

"Issie?" It was Avery, standing at the stable door. "Can I come in?"

Issie didn't say anything and Avery slid the door open and sat down beside her on the straw.

"I get the feeling that it's not just about what happened out there today with Victory, is it?" Avery said.

Issie didn't say anything for a long time. When she spoke at last, her voice was trembling. "Do you ever think about Mystic, Tom?"

Avery frowned. "That was a long time ago, Issie. What happened that day was an accident. It's got nothing to do with this…"

"But it does!" Issie said. "Don't you see? It was my fault too! I rode him out there on to the road. If I hadn't done that, Mystic would still be alive! It's all been my fault! All of it!"

"Is that what you think, Issie?" Avery's eyes suddenly welled with tears. "Is that what you've been thinking all these years, that it was your fault that he died?"

"Well, wasn't it?" Issie looked at him defiantly. "Maybe that's why it haunts me so much. I feel like Mystic is still with me. I think the truth is I can't let him go because I know deep down that it was my doing. I should never have put him in danger like that. And now Victory might die too and you expect me to ride Nightstorm around that course as well? I can't do it, Tom. I can't risk losing him like I lost Mystic…"

"Issie," Avery shook his head, "what you did that day at the pony club was extraordinarily brave. You risked your own life and saved three other horses. Mystic was just as brave. He died to save you and I think he would do it again if you gave him the chance. If he's still with you then it's not because he blames you. It's because he knows how deeply you loved him – and I truly believe that that pony loved you too."

Avery wiped the tears from Issie's face. "I know how awful the pain is of losing a horse that you truly love. I've been through it too, you know, when I lost The Soothsayer."

Issie was shocked to hear Avery speak of his horse by name. In all the years she had known him, Avery had never talked at all about The Soothsayer. He had never told her about the horrific accident that ended his career – until now.

"There'd been a lot of rain and the course was treacherous at Badminton that year," Avery said. "I was worried that he might slip going into the Vicarage Vee. I nearly took the long route but at the last minute I decided to go straight through. All I saw in my mind was glory and a clear round. If I'd known that I would lose my best horse forever…"

Avery took a deep breath. "In the aftermath of the crash I blamed myself for his death. I never rode competitively again. I didn't want to hurt another horse. I didn't want to take that enormous responsibility…"

Avery looked hard at Issie. "But I know now that I was wrong. The Soothsayer's death wasn't my fault. It was a freak accident. And giving up my riding career didn't bring him back – in the same way that your quitting now won't help Victory to recover. You won't achieve anything by giving up, Issie. But if you can find the courage in yourself to get back on your horse and get out there and ride this course, then you will honour the memory of Mystic. You owe him that at least, don't you?"

As they sat there together on the straw, Issie felt the warm touch of a horse's muzzle against her bare skin.

She looked up and saw Storm, standing right there beside her. The stallion was looking intently at her as if to say, "This is my decision too, you know. We're partners, you and I. And this isn't over yet!"

Issie reached out a hand and softly stroked the stallion's velvet nose. Then, wrapping both her hands in Storm's mane, she held on tight and the big, bay raised his neck, lifting her up off the floor and on to her feet.

As she stood there with her arms around her horse, Issie realised that she had a choice to make. Avery had let the past destroy his career. But she had another chance now, a chance to make things right.

Issie turned back to face Tom, her eyes shining, not with tears but with hope. "Tell Stella to start tacking him up. I'm going back to the truck to get ready."

As Issie got dressed, there was one last bitter reminder of what she had been through already that day. Her airtech jacket was now discarded, spent and useless. She needed to borrow another one and fast.

When Issie turned up on Marcus Pearce's doorstep with her eyes still red from crying, he didn't ask any stupid questions and never mentioned the accident. Marcus had the common sense to realise that what she needed right now was to stay positive about the task ahead. He handed over an airtech jacket. "Hey," he said. "I'm worried that Velluto Rosso might not pass the trotting-up tomorrow. Do you think Natasha might have a pair of jodhpurs I can wear to distract the judges?"

Issie laughed. "I don't think she's designing them for boys just yet."

A bit of banter with Marcus was just what Issie needed to get her emotions back on track. She had to go into the cross-country start box in an upbeat and focused state of mind. She had to put the past behind her. Her mindset had to be about bringing Storm over that finish line with a clear round and a good time.

In the warm-up area Stella and Avery kept their own worries well hidden as they helped Issie to prepare. Stella was all smiles as she did the last gear check on Nightstorm and gave him the thumbs up for Issie to get onboard.

"Storm's totally ready to do this," she said to Issie. "He was so excited he wouldn't stay still when I was tacking him up."

Issie adjusted her helmet, tightened the Velcro on her gloves and did a final check on her stopwatch. "Well, let's not keep him waiting any longer," she said to Stella. "Let's do it."

In the start box the steward held her back, waiting until the voices at the other end of his walkie-talkie confirmed that the track ahead was clear.

"You're good to go," the steward said at last. "Are you ready?"

Issie nodded and took up a tight grip on Storm's reins. The stallion knew it was time – every muscle in his body was tensed as they approached the line.

"On your marks, get set and… go!"

The electronic timer peeped as Issie and Nightstorm shot forward. They were off on the Burghley cross-country and as they took a clean leap over the hayfeeder, Issie urged the stallion on and tried to get his gallop in a strong rhythm. In her mind, she was already preparing for the next jump and the next one. And as she took each one on a perfect forward stride she was counting them down, ticking them off the list. Four fences down, only twenty-six to come…

By the time they reached fence five, the trakehner, Issie could already feel how much stronger the stallion was than Victory had been at this point. She'd been worried that his leg injury and the box rest had affected his fitness, but if anything Storm was fitter and faster than he'd ever been before. They had ridden over a kilometre at a flat gallop and taken some enormous fences and the big bay wasn't even breathing hard yet.

"Tragedy this morning for Issie Brown with her first ride," Mike Partridge intoned over the loudspeakers, "but look at the way she's bouncing back! It has been a textbook round so far on this stunning bay stallion!"

"Absolutely, Mike," Jilly Jones agreed with her co-announcer. "Just watch how this young girl approaches the fences on a loose rein – it shows her absolute faith in Nightstorm. They're at fence eleven now – the Elephant Trap – and my goodness, this big bay stallion just made that enormous spread look like a trotting pole!"

They might have been making the fences look easy, but Issie wasn't taking anything for granted. She rode

Nightstorm carefully and precisely into the Cheddar Corner, expertly managing to hold her line through the tight angles of the fences over undulating terrain, and then urging her horse on to the big log and down through the road and back up to jump The Point.

As they came in to the hedge and waterfall, Issie checked her minute marker. Storm's gallop had been swift and steady, but when she looked at her stopwatch she was disappointed to see that they were precisely on time. If they slowed down in the slightest, or took a long route at any of the jumps then they would finish outside the time for sure.

As they came in to the long gallop that led to the Centaur's Leap, Issie realised that they would have to take the short route all the way if they wanted to make the time. And that included through The Grove.

She was about to press Nightstorm on to gallop harder, when she felt her left leg suddenly collapse beneath her!

Taken totally by surprise, Issie looked down and saw her stirrup iron dangling from her left foot, the leather trailing below it. Her stirrup buckle must have snapped completely and her stirrup had fallen off the saddle!

Shaking her foot to rid it of the now-useless iron, she tried to figure out what to do. Her left leg had nothing to hold it up. It was dangling like a rag doll.

Still moving at a gallop, Issie looked up ahead and saw the Centaur's Leap looming on the horizon. In less than two hundred metres she was about to face the biggest fence on the course. And she was riding with just one stirrup!

A jump like that was ridiculously hard to handle at the best of times – but with a missing stirrup it was impossible.

After all Issie had been through, she was forced to admit defeat because of something as basic and stupid as a broken stirrup leather? It was too cruel. Too awful.

They were still galloping and were only a hundred metres away from the jump. Issie needed to pull up if she was going to stop Storm safely in time. She looked down at her left leg, dangling uselessly. She had no stirrup – it was insane to continue!

She gathered up her reins, ready to pull Nightstorm up to a halt. But something in her heart stopped her from pulling back. And not just her own heart but also the heart of this horse who galloped on so boldly beneath her. At that moment, Issie realised she did have a choice. It was risky, it was foolhardy and it was totally crazy. But she was doing it anyway. Taking a firm grip on the reins, she dug both heels into Storm's sides and urged him on once more – heading full tilt at the fence. She was attacking the Centaur's Leap with just one stirrup. They were going to jump.

CHAPTER 14

It was a moment of madness, but it was too late to back out now. Issie was committed to the jump. Focusing her eyes at the top of the hedge she pushed Nightstorm on with her legs. The stallion took a massive stride and flung himself over the ditch. Issie kept her eyes ahead and tried to ignore the chasm beneath them, jamming her knees into the saddle pads to keep her position. A fall halfway over this fence would be catastrophic!

Clearing the ditch and the hedge, Storm landed heavily on the other side. As his hind legs jolted down, Issie was jerked forward. She braced against the kneepads to keep her balance without both stirrups to anchor her.

It wasn't until Nightstorm had put in a couple of strides and was galloping once more that she realised that they were over. She'd cleared the Centaur's Leap on one stirrup!

Now that the fence was behind her, Issie knew she had to face reality. There were still more than a dozen fences to come! As Nightstorm galloped on she told herself that she should pull up and retire, but up ahead she could see The Grove looming. Perhaps she could get over just one more fence before she gave up?

As she galloped into the last hundred metres before The Grove Issie thought just how crazy this was. She was about to jump a complex of fences that she had failed to clear when she attempted it on Victory. And she'd had both stirrups that time!

In a way though, having no stirrups worked in her favour. She was so preoccupied with simply staying in the saddle that she didn't have time to panic or reflect on the past.

She rode at the fence on a bold stride and was forced to throw her weight back to counterbalance the lost stirrup as Nightstorm popped the bank and then put in a perfect stride and neatly took the last hedge, before picking up his pace again straight away on the other side and galloping on strongly.

"Look at this incredible performance!" Jilly Jones was overwhelmed. "Isadora Brown is riding this course with just one stirrup! How on earth she is managing to stay on over these fences is utterly beyond me!"

Out on the course, the crowds had been alerted to the fact that a rider was surviving the course somehow with just one stirrup. The spectators crowded the barriers trying to get a glimpse of this girl and everywhere Issie went a cheer would rise up as they urged her to keep going.

This is bonkers! I should pull up now, Issie thought as she headed towards the round tops. *There's no way we can handle a combination like this on one stirrup.*

But Storm was galloping so boldly, and as she got closer to the fence, it seemed unfair to stop him. She saw a perfect stride a few metres out and pressed on. Hup-one and hup-two! The round tops were behind her and she was galloping on to the next jump, the downhill bounce.

"She's still going!" Mike Partridge was amazed. "And look at the way she's riding between the fences too!

She's tucking her leg up and into the saddle so that all her weight is on her knee and the horse is free to gallop. And this horse is certainly galloping hard! I don't imagine this young rider cares about the time on the clock though – she just wants to make it around this course."

Mike Partridge was right. Issie had stopped bothering to look at her watch. She remained on the verge of giving up and after each and every jump she told herself that this was enough, that it was madness to continue and that she should stop now before they crashed or she fell from sheer exhaustion. But every time a new fence loomed Storm seemed to come at it on such a perfect stride and everything felt so right. *Keep going,* the voice in her head was telling her. *You're nearly there. Take him home, take him home…*

At the water complex Storm dived in so fast she was blinded by water splash but somehow she pulled him back and set him up again in time for the jump out which was followed by a bounce and then a very narrow flowerbox. It wasn't the most elegant performance but she stayed onboard. After that there was a tight turn to set her up on a straight line to the 29th fence, The Sofa, and then, before she knew it, Issie was heading for the last fence, The Orb – a round enclosed jump with the words Burghley Horse Trials printed on the banner above the horse's head.

As Storm jumped through the Orb, she forced her aching left leg up and jammed her knee into the saddle pad so that she could lever herself up off Storm's back into jockey position for the final gallop over the last two hundred metres. Using the very last vestiges of strength in her tired body, she stayed tucked up above the saddle one last time and urged the stallion on as hard as she could with her hands driving him for home. As they flew across the finish line an enormous roar of support rose up from the Burghley crowd for their one-stirruped clear round. Issie had made it! She was home and she was clear, but there was no way they could have been galloping fast enough to make it home within the time. There would be time faults – there had to be!

Bracing herself for the worst, she looked down at her stopwatch. She'd pressed it as she crossed the line and the timer was fixed on fifteen minutes exactly! Was her watch right? Had she really made it in time?

"Issie! Ohmygod! Issie!" Stella came running towards

her and the look on her best friend's face made Issie realise that there was no mistake. She had done it! They had made the time on the cross-country. It was a clear round.

"A cross-country round that will go down in Burghley history as one of the most heart-stopping ever!" raved Mike Partridge over the loudspeakers.

"Issie Brown has made it home in the allocated time, riding almost half the course on just one stirrup!"

The incredible performance was the talk of Burghley. With just the showjumping round still to come tomorrow, Issie Brown had held her lead and stayed in contention to take out the coveted Grand Slam.

But it was too early for celebrations, and once the excitement died away The Laurels's team were back in serious work mode once again. The loss of the stirrup meant more than just trouble on the cross-country course. It could also mean disastrous consequences still to come.

"You did a great job staying onboard and getting him around clear," Avery told Issie, "but it's not over yet.

You were really bouncing around out there and it's possible that he's sustained a muscle strain from the ride or gone lame. We could be in real trouble in the trotting-up tomorrow."

Normally Issie would have been perched up on her stirrups for support to stay off Storm's back when he galloped between jumps, but because she had lost one stirrup, she had been unable to stop herself from coming down with a thud in the saddle several times on the course. Had she accidentally injured her horse in the process? If he turned out to be lame at the trot-up tomorrow morning he would be 'spun' – the judges would eliminate him before she even had a chance to ride the showjumping phase. She needed Nightstorm sound and fit to pass the trot-up with flying colours and compete tomorrow.

"I'm sorry, I can't guarantee that," Stella said when Issie visited the stables that evening.

"Storm's got heat in his lower legs – there's some tissue damage but that's absolutely typical after a hard cross-country. I'm changing ice boots on all four legs every twenty minutes. And I've been massaging his shoulders and back with liniment. But at the moment it's impossible to say if he'll pass the trot-up. Right now, I'd say it's fifty-fifty. I'm doing everything I can but it's a case of wait and see."

Stella saw the mortified expression on Issie's face. "I wish I had better news, Issie, but I won't lie to you. Storm had a rough time out there today. If he were any other horse he would have pulled up dead lame – but he's tough, he's a fighter. And I'm doing everything I can."

"What can I do?" Issie asked.

"You can go back to the truck and get some sleep," Stella told her. "I've got things covered here. There's nothing more you can do to help him right now."

Issie did as Stella said. She went back to the horse truck with Avery and did her very best to keep her strength up for tomorrow by forcing herself to swallow down some dinner and going straight to bed. But she couldn't sleep. She lay down in her cot bed in the back of the truck and thought about everything that had happened that day. They'd had a call just before dinner from Kate who told them that Victory had arrived safely in Glasgow and after a thorough examination the vets had declared him a perfect candidate for surgery. The brown gelding was due in theatre the next morning for the three-hour operation.

It seemed that all Issie could do was wait. Wait for Kate's call after the op, and wait until tomorrow morning when the trotting-up would reveal her future. If Storm was sound, then they would be allowed into the showjumping ring. If not, it would be the end of their dream.

Sleep was virtually impossible under the circumstances. Issie tried her best but by six in the morning, having grabbed only a couple of hours at the most, she gave up and headed down to the stables. Stella was there with Storm, ice-packing his legs one last time.

"How is he?" Issie asked.

Stella shook her head. "I honestly don't know," she admitted. "I've been working on him for most of the night, but it's going to be touch and go. He's still a little stiff and his action is compromised. I'm positive that he's not sore – but I can't explain that to the judges. They'll have to look at him and make up their own minds."

Judging whether a horse is actually lame or not isn't always easy and it requires an expert eye. In the case of the Burghley Horse Trials it required six eyes. There would be three judges watching as the horses were presented.

The crowds, as usual, were out in force to watch the trotting-up. There was a cheer as Issie stepped up to the line, ready to trot Storm for the judges, but she found it impossible to muster a smile for the assembled spectators under the circumstances.

She was terrified that Nightstorm would fail. She tried to stay calm when the steward gave her the nod to take her turn.

"Come on, Storm!" Issie jiggled the lead rope and Storm broke into a trot beside her as she sprinted gracefully down the length of hard tarmac, his hooves chiming out alongside her.

At the end of the tarmac strip, she turned Storm and trotted him back once more. As they passed the end of the strip the crowd cheered and clapped. And then there was stunned silence as one of the judges shook his head and called the other two judges over to confer. They stood there in deep discussion, for what seemed like an eternity and Issie could feel her heart racing as the head judge walked over to the announcer's booth. A moment later, the voice of Mike Partridge came over the loudspeakers, solemn and grave.

"Ladies and gentlemen. I am afraid that Nightstorm has not passed."

CHAPTER 15

Back at the 'hold box', Avery did his best to keep things calm.

"It's OK," he reassured Issie. "Let's not panic. He's not spun yet."

Nightstorm might have failed his first round, but he wasn't out. The procedure for the trot-up was very exact and at this stage Nightstorm had been turned down by the judges – but that didn't mean he'd been spun.

The first stage of disqualification was being sent to the 'hold box'. This was where Storm was now. He hadn't passed the trot-up but he hadn't actually failed it yet either. A second inspection would take place, this time with a vet called in to check the horse, and then

Nightstorm would be presented to the judges once again. Then and only then, if he didn't pass a second time, Nightstorm would be spun and eliminated.

In the hold box, Issie tried to stay calm while Stella felt Storm's legs for any residual signs of heat and put ice packs on while they waited for the vet to arrive.

"Are you sure he's OK?" Issie asked her. "I don't want to ride him if he's in any pain. If you think he's unsound I'll pull out now…"

Stella shook her head. "There's nothing wrong with him as far as I can tell. He's just a little stiff. If you ask me, the judge who put him in the hold box is just playing it safe – they can't believe you could get round the course with him on one stirrup and he'd still be sound the next day!"

When the vet arrived moments later he said the same thing as Stella. "Present him again," the vet insisted.

Issie's heart was pounding as she led Storm back to the judges for the second time that morning. A hush fell over the crowd as Nightstorm began his trot and all you could hear was the choc-choc of his metal horseshoes clacking against the hard tarmac as he trotted one way and then turned and trotted back again.

As the judges conferred a second time, Issie held her breath. Then the head judge stepped forward and gave her the nod. The result this time was unanimous. Nightstorm was passed as fit, sound and ready to compete!

It was midday when the showjumping finally got underway. Mike Partridge was in the announcer's box with Jilly Jones and she was explaining the running order of a three-day event showjumping class to the crowd in the packed stadium. "We're working our way through the riders in reverse order through the rankings," Jilly said. "Our last partnership in the arena today will be the combination currently at the very top of the leaderboard, Isadora Brown on Nightstorm. They sit on their dressage score of 37."

Seventy-four riders had begun the competition at Burghley on Friday. Now, after eliminations of one kind or another, only thirty-three were left to compete in this final phase. That meant that thirty-two riders had to take their turn in the arena before Issie got her chance to ride.

As the first rider cantered into the arena, Issie was still back at the horse truck eating lunch. She wouldn't be competing for another two hours and there was no point in making herself nervous by standing around in the stadium and watching the other competitors.

After lunch she took her time getting dressed. Her showjumping kit was laid out and waiting for her, a short black jacket, pure white jodhpurs and long shiny black boots. She was just adjusting her hairnet in the mirror when there was a knock at the horse-truck door. Issie opened it and got the shock of her life. There was a woman on her doorstep, her hair a tumbling mess of blonde curls. She was dressed in a white cotton dress, her throat and wrists weighed down with loads of gold jewellery.

"Ohmygod! Aunty Hess!"

"Oh what a relief!" Hester threw her arms around her niece. "You're still here! We just saw Tom at the stables and he said you were probably back at the truck. We were hoping to catch you and wish you luck before you went into the ring."

"We?" Issie looked puzzled. Who else was here with her aunt?

Then Issie caught sight of the dark-haired woman standing behind Hester on the stairs and let out a shriek of joy.

"Mum!"

Mrs Brown bounded up and gave her daughter a massive hug. "We've been looking all over for you. The security guards were very uptight about letting us into the stables. They didn't seem to care when I said that I was your mother."

Hester waved the lanyard that she was wearing around her neck. "Well, it's all sorted now," she said. "Tom gave us these VIP swing tags so that we can go anywhere we want. Apparently they'll get us into the good seats to watch you when you're jumping."

"I'd have organised that for you, but I wasn't sure if you were coming," Issie said.

Issie's mum had long ago given up on coming to watch her daughter ride. Mrs Brown found it so terrifying standing there helplessly on the sidelines as her only child tackled the enormous fences, she simply wasn't brave enough to do it. Instead, she usually watched the action on the TV in the hotel room so she could muffle her squeals with a pillow when things got too scary for her. But last night when Issie phoned to tell her mum about the traumatic events on the cross-country course, Mrs Brown knew that she needed to steel her nerves and be there this time. Her daughter needed her support.

"How many rails do you have in hand going into the showjumping?" Mrs Brown asked.

"Amanda!" Hester teased her. "You almost sound like you know what you're talking about. Since when did you become so horsey?"

Issie smiled at her mum's new-found mastery of showjumping talk. "I can only afford to drop one rail," she told them. "Jenny Rathbone is right behind me on Mr Marmaduke. There's only five points between us."

"Well, I don't want to jinx anything by wishing you luck," Hester said, "so I'll just say break a leg instead…"

As soon as the words came out Hester realised what she had done.

Everyone had gone out of their way not to mention the tragedy of Victory's horrible accident in front of Issie today. She needed to concentrate on staying positive and focused. But now that Hester had said it there was no way of taking the words back. Issie's face turned as pale as a sheet.

"How is Victory doing?" Mrs Brown asked gently, no longer avoiding the subject. "Has there been any news?"

Issie shook her head. "He should have been out of theatre by now. Kate said she would phone us as soon as they knew anything but she still hasn't called."

Issie was really worried.

"If they find that the leg can't be successfully mended then that will be the end," Kate had told Issie when they last spoke. "They won't wake him up again. They'll put him down while he's asleep on the operating table – it's the kindest thing to do."

That last phone call from Kate had been hours ago. Surely the surgery was over by now? Or had it gone so badly that Kate was afraid to call? Issie had been trying so hard to push it out of her mind, and focus on the showjumping, but now Hester's innocent mistake had unravelled all of that and Issie felt worry tying her tummy in knots.

She walked with Hester and her mum to meet Stella

and Avery at the warm-up arena. Stella handed her Nightstorm's reins and Issie handed Stella her mobile.

"Kate promised to call me as soon as she had news," she told Stella. "Can you answer it for me? I want to know as soon as they come out of theatre."

Stella saw the anxiety in Issie's eyes. She took the mobile, clasping it tightly in her hand. "As soon as I hear from her I'll tell you straight away. Now stop worrying! You've got a showjumping course to think about!"

Issie had walked the showjumping course that morning with Avery, who had declared it one of the most testing that he had ever seen at a three-day event. There were thirteen fences in total – including a double and treble combination.

The course had caused trouble for many riders that day and by the time Issie was mounted up to watch the last few competitors attempt their rounds, the scoreboard registered the complexity of the track.

"Another eight faults for Nina Bennington on Lucite Dynamite," Mike Partridge told the crowd in the stands. "This is proving to be a very intricate course this year."

"Indeed it is, Mike," Jilly Jones agreed. "There are some tight twists and turns and the time penalties have caused trouble too."

In the main arena now Marcus Pearce was doing better than most. He was performing a brilliant round on Velluto Rosso. As they charged at the Liverpool, Velluto Rosso took a leap from too far back, causing the crowd to gasp, but they made it over and Marcus rode the liver chestnut mare perfectly over the double and the final fence leaving all the rails intact.

"Which currently puts them in sixth place," Jilly Jones said, "although they could rise up the rankings if anyone ahead of them makes a mistake."

The next rider entered the arena, but Issie didn't stay to watch. There were only another four riders to come and then it would be her turn. She needed to go and warm up.

As she trotted Nightstorm around the warm-up arena she could feel the tiredness in her horse, the stiffness in his legs as he took each stride. She would have to be careful around this complicated course. They had one rail in hand.

Luckily that one rail didn't include the warm-up fence or their chances would have been ruined before they even began!

Nightstorm had an attack of clumsiness the first time that Issie tried to take him over the practice jump. He took three strides to the fence then chipped in a fourth stride and leapt awkwardly at the last moment, taking out the top two rails!

"It's OK, boy, it doesn't matter." Issie settled the stallion down as she looked at the fallen rails they had left in their wake. But inside she was tensing up. What if Storm was too tired to handle the showjumps today? His timing had never been off like that before. Issie kept the stallion in a canter and came around in a loop to try once more. This time Storm backed off at the last minute and tried to jump from too far back, demolishing the fence completely with his chest as he ploughed through it!

Avery saw the distress on Issie's face and came over to talk to her.

"You're both rattled," he said. "Just leave the warm-up

jump. Forget about it. Walk him around a bit and calm down before you get called in."

Issie only had another minute or two to calm her nerves before the stewards were calling her over to the ring. In the main arena Jenny Rathbone and Mr Marmaduke were finishing their round. They were just coming up to the double which they took with ease. The crowd let out a gasp as Mr Marmaduke scraped a rail on the very last jump and the pole rocked in its cups – but it didn't fall!

"And that really puts the pressure on!" Jilly Jones trilled. "Jenny Rathbone finishes clear on a final score of forty-two which means that our last competitor of the day, Isadora Brown, can only afford one rail down if she wants to win at Burghley."

As Issie and Nightstorm entered the arena the thousands of onlookers in the stands seemed to hold their breath in unison. Everyone here understood how important this round was and they didn't dare to talk, cough or utter a word that might disrupt the thoughts of the young rider who was now circling her magnificent bay stallion around the perimeter of the arena. Even Mike Partridge lowered his voice to a reverential whisper as he addressed the crowds.

"Just seventeen years old," Mike Partridge took up the commentary, "and what a whirlwind rise to superstardom! First among equals at the four-star horse trials in Kentucky on a chance ride from the Valmont Stables, a mare named Liberty. Then she covered herself in glory at the Badminton Horse Trials on the Australian Thoroughbred, Victory."

At the mention of Victory's name, Issie felt herself tense up. She still hadn't heard from Kate! Was the brown gelding going to pull through? *Don't think about it, Issie, keep your head in the game.*

"And here she is," Mike Partridge continued, "with just one rail in hand, riding on her own homebred stallion, a horse with a Spanish sire and an Anglo-Arabian dam, who grew up in Chevalier Point in New Zealand..." Mike Partridge paused as the bell rang, signalling that Issie had just one minute before she had to begin her round.

"This young talent faces enormous pressure," Mike Partridge told the crowd. "If she wins this competition, Issie Brown takes home not just Burghley, but also the coveted $350,000 prize that is the Grand Slam. She has everything to ride for – and everything to lose!"

Knowing that the clock was ticking and she needed to pass through the flags within the next minute, Issie took one last loop, cantering right around the jumps. As she circled, she took a look at the spectators in the stands. There were thousands of them watching her, and hundreds of thousands around the world in front of their televisions, all waiting to see if she could achieve the fabled Grand Slam. She should have been nervous, but as she cantered around to ride through the flags, she felt Storm collect his stride beneath her, his canter becoming energised and bouncy, and a surge of confidence ran through her. A moment ago this horse had felt tired and battle-weary, but in front of the crowds in the arena he suddenly came alive. It was as if the great stallion knew that the thousands of spectators were here just to see him – and he was rising to the occasion.

"C'mon," Issie said to her horse, "let's show them what you've got."

Fence number one was the Burghley Towers, a grey castle with lightweight wooden bricks at the top that had got the better of many of the day's competitors. But not Nightstorm. He flew the fence with a clean pair of heels on a perfect forward stride and Issie sat back straight away already looking to the next fence, an upright, balancing him back before she saw the stride and sent him on.

"Beautifully ridden over fences one and two," Jilly Jones took up the commentary. "This girl sets up the horse so neatly and just lets the jump come to her. They've got such a natural relationship, these two – look at Nightstorm's ears pivoting as he comes into a fence. He's listening to everything this girl on his back is saying to him…".

Jilly Jones was right. Storm was listening – and Issie was talking to him non-stop, reassuring him the whole way.

"This one is easy, another stride, come on! Good boy!" She coaxed him over fence three, another upright, and then a parallel followed by a tight turn to a very tight upright again and then the sloping rails of the Swedish oxer.

As the course twisted and turned, Issie and Storm seemed to dance their way from jump to jump, every movement fluid and graceful, always on the perfect stride.

But if they made it look easy, the truth was that these fences were taking every last scrap of power and strength that the pair had left. At the parallel, Issie felt the bay stallion really exert himself to get enough air between him and the fence and she heard his grunt as he landed. He was tiring and she was exhausted; they were hanging on, but could they make it to the end of this difficult course?

At the treble everything went wrong at the first element when they took off from too far back and Issie had to push Storm to make the stallion put in a mammoth stride to take the second fence and then collect up again to get over the third. As they landed, she heard his hind hoof ping against one of the coloured poles. Issie listened for the crash but it never came. They were over the treble and they were still clear, and now over the bridge and the big parallel – clear and clear again!

"Only three fences to go, one rail still in hand!" Mike Partridge reminded the crowd as Issie and Nightstorm set themselves up for the Liverpool.

They were over that. Issie's heart was in her mouth as she approached the double. Hup-one and hup-two!

They were through! There was only one fence still to come and as they galloped down on it far too fast she was talking to the bay stallion all the way. "One more, boy," she urged him on. "You can do it!"

Storm took off and they were in the air, soaring over the last jump and then down on the other side and through the flags. They had done it! Not a single pole had fallen! They finished on a clear round with no time penalties to remain on an incredible score of 37!

As they raced through the flags, Issie ripped off her riding helmet and waved it wildly in the air to the crowds who were going wild with excitement.

"A standing ovation, and well deserved!" Mike Partridge cried, "because this young rider from Chevalier Point has just made history here at Burghley... Isadora Brown has won the Grand Slam!"

CHAPTER 16

The prize-giving was preceded by a display by the Belvoir Hounds, who were escorted around the arena by the hunt master in a red coat on a strapping grey Irish Hunter.

In the official ceremony that followed, the top five riders entered the ring on horseback with Nightstorm leading the way. Storm wore his navy wool winner's rug adorned with the Burghley logo draped over his saddle and a wreath of white roses around his neck. He seemed particularly pleased about the wreath and gave Issie a sideways look as if to say, "Don't try to take this off me – I'll be eating these back at the stables later."

The riders dismounted to receive their awards and

Issie watched as Marcus Pearce stepped forward to receive his prize on Velluto Rosso. Marcus had put in a remarkable cross-country and showjumping round to hold his score and when two of the riders ahead of him had dropped a pole in the final phase he shot up the leaderboard to finish in fourth place.

Marcus looked solemn and formal as he bowed regally to the Marquess. Then he looked over at Issie and gave her a wink which almost made her burst into a fit of giggles and she had to work very hard to compose herself before her turn came to step forward and accept the silver Burghley platter.

Holding the trophy in one hand, she turned around waving to the crowds, smiling up at the thousands of spectators who were on their feet, giving the winner of the Grand Slam a standing ovation.

As Issie left the arena, she saw Stella in the wings waving frantically to her with a huge grin on her face. She thought that Stella was excited about the ceremony. It wasn't until the redhead began running towards her that Issie realised it was more than that. "I've just had a call from Kate," Stella told her. "The operation took longer than they expected and it was complicated…"

she looked at Issie, her eyes shining. "But it turned out brilliantly. Victory made it! He's going to be just fine!"

It was late that evening when Avery guided the horse truck down the tree-lined driveway that led to the stables at The Laurels.

It felt like a lifetime ago that they had left the farm, but it had only been five days. As Avery pulled the truck to a stop in front of the yard Issie leapt out of the cab and lowered the back, jumping in to lead Nightstorm out. When he got to the bottom of the ramp the stallion paused and raised his magnificent head and let out a loud whinny.

"The winner of the Grand Slam is announcing his arrival!" Francoise emerged from the stable block to give Issie a double-cheeked kiss.

"Don't let it go to your head, Storm," Issie warned as she led him to his stall. "You're not getting any special treatment around here just because you've won the Burghley Horse Trials."

The stables were almost full that evening. Francoise had two of her young eventers in the stalls next to Nightstorm, and in the box furthest away from the stallion was the chestnut mare, Mirabelle.

"She is still in foal!" Francoise said with obvious frustration. "If I had known that she would wait this long then I would have come and watched you at Burghley! She was due a week ago – look at the size of her belly!"

Mirabelle's tummy was enormous – but the mare showed no signs of foaling any time soon. She was happily munching on her hay net and looked quite content.

Francoise filled Issie in on the progress of the two young eventers. "Leonardo is jumping beautifully. We'll work on his dressage tomorrow. I have entered you for the Weston Park two-star this weekend."

"This weekend!" Issie said. "Francoise, I thought I might take a little break! I've just won the Grand Slam!"

"The horses do not care about your trophies," Francoise informed her. "They still need work. The young ones need you most of all, they will be your future."

Issie knew this was true. All the same, she had been

hoping that Francoise would at least allow her a moment of celebration before she put her nose to the grindstone again.

"A good rider is always looking to the next fence," Francoise reminded her as they walked back to the house together. "You never know what you will have to confront next…"

As she said this, Francoise opened the door to the kitchen and Issie saw a huge hand-painted banner strung right across the room with the words *Wham! Bam! Grand Slam!* in giant letters. Beneath the banner was a table covered with plates of food and standing at the front of it, holding a large iced cake, was Avery with Mrs Brown, Hester, Stella, Kate and Marcus.

"Surprise!" Stella said.

"Ohmygod!" Issie looked around the room at her friends. "I had no idea you were going to do this!"

"Well, duh!" Stella said. "That's why it's called a surprise party!"

"You did not think we would let this moment pass by without at least a little party," Francoise laughed. "Come on, cut the cake!"

The celebrations went on until very late.

"We deserve at least one night off from our training schedules," Marcus told her, "don't you think?"

Marcus had news of his own. After his performance at Burghlcy the owners of Velluto Rosso had decided to offer him the ride permanently, and they were moving two of their other horses to the Goldins' stables where Marcus would base himself for the next few seasons.

"We're going to be neighbours," Marcus told her.

"You can pop in and borrow a cup of hard feed," Issie replied.

"I'll take you up on that offer," Marcus said.

It was after midnight when the party finally broke up. Issie stayed up to help Francoise with the dishes. The enormous quantities of food seemed to have somehow magically disappeared, although there was still a slice of carrot cake left. "Storm can have this piece," Issie said, wrapping the cake in a napkin. "He's earnt it."

The night air had a hint of autumn chill as she

walked down the path that led to the stable block. Storm must have heard her coming because he was waiting for her with his head over the door. When he spied the cake in her hands he gave a keen nicker. Issie fed him the treat and giggled at the expression on Storm's face as he was overwhelmed by the sweetness of the icing. He shook his head up and down, his eyes wide.

"There's carrots in it," Issie reassured him, "so it's still healthy."

She stood there for a while, leaning over the door, not saying a word, admiring the conformation of the big bay, the way his muscles rippled beneath his shining coat as he moved around in the loose box. It would take him a few weeks to recover completely from the rigours of the past few days, but then they would be back on the circuit again. The Olympics were looming on the horizon and there was the four-star in Adelaide coming up too – it would be fun to fly Storm to Australia to compete and they had the funds to do it now. Already their old sponsors Dashing Equine and GG Feeds were muttering about coming back onboard. Not that the Laurels team needed to worry about sponsorship money too much with the winnings of the Grand Slam soon to be in their coffers.

The official presentation of the Grand Slam trophy – and the accompanying cheque for $350,000 – was scheduled for next week. Maybe then it would all feel real to her, but right now Issie was still in a state of shock. She couldn't believe that she had taken out the greatest prize in the world of eventing. And yet, when she looked at the magnificent bay stallion in front of her, she had the sense that her partnership with Storm hadn't reached its potential. There were more adventures to come, she knew that for certain.

Issie was still gazing at Storm when she heard a bang. The noise didn't worry her at first. It was a horse kicking out, hooves striking against the door of the loose box. Perhaps one of the young geldings was throwing a tantrum, demanding more dinner. It wasn't until she heard a second bang, and an accompanying distraught whinny, that Issie suddenly realised which loose box it was coming from.

Ohmygod! Mirabelle!

In just a few seconds Issie had sprinted down the row to reach the mare. Mirabelle must have been standing up a moment ago when she kicked out, but now she had collapsed on the straw, her rump facing the door. She was in labour. Issie could tell from the way the mare kept turning her head to look at her flank, giving little grunts of pain and then collapsing down on the straw again.

Entering the box and rebolting it, Issie gently eased her way alongside Mirabelle, talking softly to the mare as she edged around until she was close enough to examine the foal monitor that the mare was wearing around her neck. The device was supposed to alert Francoise that the mare was foaling, but it hadn't activated and by the looks of things, the foal wasn't far away. Mares could give birth very quickly.

Issie had decided that the best thing to do was to run back up to the house to get Francoise, when she noticed something underneath Mirabelle's tail. The foal was already beginning to come. Issie could see the slimy, opaque membrane sac that encased the foal poking out from beneath the mare's tail.

Issie had seen a mare give birth before. She'd been there the night that Storm was born, and as soon as she looked at this foal she knew something was very different about this delivery.

Foals usually came out of the mare front legs first. But this foal's legs were sticking up at a weird angle.

At first, Issie thought the legs were malformed, but, as the mare gave a grunt and the legs pushed out further from beneath her tail, Issie realised that the legs weren't abnormal – they were the *hind legs*. The foal was being born hindquarters first.

Issie's heart began to race. Foals weren't supposed to be born like this! They usually came out with their heads tucked in between their front legs. Once the shoulder was clear, they slipped out very quickly into a wet bundle on the straw. But occasionally, you got a foal that came out back-to-front like this one – and then things got really complicated.

Issie's heart pounded. Foals that were born this way could get stuck. The mare could panic and the risks suddenly became very real for both mother and foal. Mirabelle needed a vet to deliver her foal safely. Issie needed to get Francoise and Kate – now.

"It's OK, girl," Issie reassured the mare. "Everything's going to be OK, but I have to go and get help. I'm going to have to leave you on your own for a while. I can't do this alone…"

Issie stood up and stepped back towards the door. Turning around to open it, she leapt back in shock. A horse's head was hanging over the loose box door, staring straight at her!

"Ohmygod!" Issie gasped.

It was Mystic. The grey gelding was standing at the door like a marble statue, his coal-black eyes shining as he stood calm and serene, watching over the scene in the stables.

He looked at Issie and in that moment she knew that she wasn't going anywhere. It was as if the grey pony was holding her there with his presence, willing her to stay with the ailing mare. There was no time left, not for the vet or even Francoise. If Issie left now the mare or foal could be dead by the time she got back. If Mirabelle was going to get her foal out alive, Issie would have to be the one to do it.

Lowering herself down beside Mirabelle's hindquarters, Issie kept talking gently to the mare as she took a closer look at the legs inside the membrane sac. Her heart sank. This foal was definitely coming out hind legs first, and there was no time to lose. The longer the foal was trapped at this point, the more risk there was for Mirabelle and her baby.

Getting up again, Issie moved around to the mare's head. "C'mon!" she said firmly, grasping Mirabelle by the halter. "You need to get up."

Mares often delivered their foals lying down, but when a foal was jammed in tight, with its legs stuck, the only way to get them out was to stick your hands in and pull. And Issie wasn't strong enough to do that if Mirabelle was on the ground – she needed gravity on her side.

Mirabelle didn't want to stand up at first. The mare was in too much pain and she fought against Issie's tugs. But Issie persevered and pulled harder on the halter, growling encouragement at Mirabelle until finally the mare heaved the weight of her enormous belly up off the straw beneath her and got up on her feet.

"Good girl!" Issie praised her. "We're going to get the foal out, you and me. We can do this, Mirabelle!"

Issie wasn't sure who she was trying to reassure, the mare or herself. Taking a deep breath and rolling her sleeves up, she moved around to the rear of the mare and stroked her rump.

"I'm right here, Mirabelle," she reassured the mare. "Don't kick me, OK?"

If Mirabelle kicked out in fright Issie wouldn't be able to get out of the way of her flying hooves. Luckily, even though the mare was anxious, she seemed to realise that Issie was trying to help her. Issie stuck out both hands and grasped the membrane sac. It was rubbery and warm, and extremely gooey. Her hands slipped across it, trying to get a grip as she felt along the length of the foal's leg until she reached what felt like a hock. She couldn't see what she was touching and was relying completely on feel. Mirabelle kept turning her head to sniff at her flank, but she didn't strike out as Issie managed to get both her hands clasped around what she hoped were hocks, and braced herself against the floor to pull.

Her first attempt was a little tentative. She didn't want to hurt the mare, but when nothing whatsoever happened, she prepared herself for a proper tug. This time, as she braced against the floor and heaved with all her strength the legs began to come out, slowly at first and then more easily as the rest of the membrane sac followed. Then, with one last forceful tug, everything came in a rush and the next thing Issie knew she was lying flat out on the straw, completely covered in fluid, with a squirming body on top of her! Issie had to work fast to tear open the suffocating membrane sac so that the newborn could breathe. It was surprisingly resilient but Issie ripped into it with life-or-death determination and as the membrane came apart she saw the foal properly for the very first time.

It was a colt. A beautiful baby boy. Even in his wet and bedraggled newborn state he was totally and utterly gorgeous. He had the biggest eyes Issie had ever seen, and a cute dish to his nose. As Issie tugged away the last remnants to expose the colt to the dry straw, Mirabelle began to clean her son, licking him all over with her tongue, and Issie sat back to watch as the colt tried to control his long, gangly legs and struggle to his feet.

Issie never ceased to be amazed at the way newborn horses were capable of this incredible feat – standing up on all fours within the very first hour that they were born.

She desperately wanted to lift the colt up so that he could suckle from his mother's teat, but she knew that this was something that the foal must do on his own. And so she sat and witnessed the miracle of nature as this new life staggered up on to his feet and searched out the soft belly of the mare so that he could take his first drink.

Issie's own legs seemed almost as wobbly as the foal's when she finally pushed herself up from the straw and walked over to the stable door. Mystic was still standing there, watching intently.

"They're OK," Issie said to the grey gelding. "It's all going to be OK now." The mare and the foal were going to be just fine. Mystic didn't usually linger, but this time the grey gelding seemed strangely reluctant to leave.

Issie unbolted the door and stepped out of the stall so that she was standing right next to him. She threaded her fingers through his mane, felt the warmth of his dapple-grey coat and smelt the sweet horseyness of him. Inhaling that wonderful smell, she shut her eyes tight and wrapped both arms around the neck of her beloved grey pony.

"Thank you," she whispered. "Thank you, Mystic. For everything."

It wasn't until she let go, until she felt him slip away from her fingers, that she realised she was saying goodbye. She couldn't explain it but she knew in her heart that this was the last time that she would ever see him.

"No!" Issie said, her eyes welling with tears. "I still need you."

But even as she said the words, she knew they weren't true. Mystic knew it too. So many times the grey pony had saved her, had been there to protect her. But she wasn't a little kid at Chevalier Point Pony Club any more. It was time she stepped up and started taking care of things on her own. Mystic had shown her tonight that she could do it. She had always trusted him and now, she needed to make one last leap of faith.

The tears were running down her cheeks as she looked for one last time at her grey pony, who had taken her from gymkhana to Grand Slam.

"It's OK," she nodded. "I understand. I really do."

Her love had always held him close and now at last she was ready to let him go.

The grey pony gave the girl one last look and then he turned and cantered into the darkness. Issie listened to his hoof beats as they faded away.

A moment later the lights came on in the yard and Francoise appeared at the end of the stable block. "Issie? What's going on?" Francoise saw the girl's tear-stained face and her eyes grew wide with fear. "Is Mirabelle OK?"

"She's fine," Issie said. "She's had the foal. I'll stay

with her. Can you go and wake Tom? He'll want to see this."

Francoise ran back to the house and returned minutes later with Avery at her side.

"What did she have?" Avery wanted to know. "A colt or a filly?"

"It's a colt," Issie said. "There's something about him though, Tom. I think you need to see…"

As Avery and Francoise entered the loose box and saw the colt standing on wobbly legs beside Mirabelle, they couldn't believe it.

"A grey!" Avery was surprised. "I was expecting him to be a chestnut like his mother."

Francoise shook her head in amazement. "Look! He is dark now but you can tell that his coat will be dapple one day!"

She ran her trained eyes over the colt. "I think we are looking at a future champion here," she said. "Look at that magnificent head! And those legs. He has the legs of a showjumper already!"

"Let's just hope he doesn't try to get over the jumps the way he came out of his mother!" Issie smiled. Then she told Avery and Francoise about the back-to-front birth, and how she had struggled to deliver the foal.

"These births are very dangerous," Francoise told her. "If you had not been here then the colt would not have survived. He owes you his life. I think it is only fair that you should be the one to name him."

Avery agreed. "He's your future superstar, Issie. Have you got a name for him?"

"I do," Issie said, looking at the grey foal, her eyes shining.

"His name is Mystic."

EPILOGUE

Spring weather in New Zealand is unpredictable. When Issie Brown woke up she had been expecting to see rain clouds. Instead, the skies were blue and the air was still. It was perfect hacking weather.

She came downstairs to find her mother waiting for her with scrambled eggs already on the table.

"You think I don't know what you're like?" Mrs Brown said. "I knew you'd try to dash out the door and get to that horse without eating a proper breakfast."

It had been ten years since Issie won the Grand Slam, but every time she came home her mum still treated her like a kid. Not that she was complaining. She kind of liked being fussed over – although her mum had actually ironed her jodhpurs yesterday which was a bit much.

Since her stellar win at Burghley Issie had gone on to live the glamorous life of a pro-rider, travelling the world with her horses. But not everyone had travelled with her. She had been shocked by Avery's announcement, shortly after Burghley, that he and Francoise were leaving The Laurels for good.

"We're going home to live in New Zealand," Avery told Issie. "It turns out the reason Francoise's been feeling so off-colour lately isn't the flu after all."

Francoise was expecting a baby.

"That doesn't mean you have to leave!" Issie had pointed out.

"I know that," Francoise said, "but the timing is right to go. We want to raise horses as well as a family. More future eventers like Mystic. Tom has already spoken to Cassandra Steele. She's letting us lease the stables at Dulmoth Park for our new breeding programme. We're moving back to Winterflood Farm and will keep a few of our own horses there too."

And so the Dulmoth Park horse breeding programme was established, dedicated to raising young eventers as stars of the future.

Within a few years, many of Tom and Francoise's best young horses were being sent on to The Laurels as green three-year olds to continue their schooling.

The farm in Wiltshire continued to be Issie's base in England while she competed throughout Europe. Stella Tarrant had taken over the reins as manager at The Laurels while Issie was on the road competing the advanced mounts.

It soon became more than a coincidence that at every international competition Issie seemed to find herself in the company of Marcus Pearce. They'd become best friends on the circuit, training together and helping each other whenever there was a problem with one of their horses. Issie couldn't recall the precise moment when their relationship somehow became a romance, but she would never forget that night after the final showjumping phase at Stars of Pau in France, when Marcus took her out to dinner.

Marcus had beaten Issie to first place so the dinner, at a cute little French restaurant, was his treat. At the end of the meal, Issie was digging her spoon into her crème brulee and found something shiny and rock-hard in the middle. There was a diamond ring hidden in her dessert.

"Issie," Marcus said, "I've been in love with you since the day we met. I know this is a bit of a shock, but…"

Issie stopped his speech by taking the ring, still covered in sticky custard, slipping it on her finger and kissing him.

"Yes," she said. "I'm saying yes."

They were married three years later in a ceremony at The Laurels. The bride wore an incredible white gown designed by the internationally renowned designer, Natasha Tucker.

Natasha, also a guest at the wedding, was now living the fashion life in Paris, having given up on riding to focus on clothing. Her Natty T jodhpur range was a massive success and her fortune was substantial, which suited Natasha rather nicely. Oliver Tucker's failed property deals had finally caught up with him and the last anyone heard of him he was working as a used-car salesman in Norwich.

Stella and Kate were the bridesmaids. Kate was now a fully qualified vet and had been thrilled to be offered a position working in the surgical clinic at the Glasgow Institute.

Old friends also present on the bride's side included Roberto Nunez and his son Alfonso, who had flown over from Spain for the event – and Aidan, who made the trip from New Zealand with his new girlfriend, a stunt rider called Matilda who he'd met on the set of the latest *Palomino Princess* movie.

There was no time for a honeymoon as the newlyweds were both riding at Badminton the following weekend. It was Issie's first four-star on Mystic. The grey gelding was fully grown and he stood a massive sixteen-three hands high, a true dapple-grey with coal-black eyes and a steel-grey mane.

That year the Badminton Horse Trials also marked the final competition for one of the great campaigners in Issie's stables as Comet finally bowed out of three-day eventing. Issie's other Grand Slam horse, Victory, had recovered from his leg surgery but had never been sound enough to compete again and he now lived with Kate at the Glasgow Institute.

As for Issie's most famous horse of all, Nightstorm, the years had been good to him. After he won Burghley, Nightstorm dominated the famous horse trials twice in the next five years and Badminton a record three times in total. Nightstorm's swansong had been six months ago at the Olympics in Rome.

When he was selected for the Olympic squad the critics were harsh. They said that Nightstorm was too old and too battle-weary to make it round the incredibly challenging Olympic cross-country course.

But Issie knew better. Storm was in the best form of his career – and she proved it. In Rome, the partnership went double clear to secure the individual gold medal.

Even though Storm still had a lot of gas left in his tank – and was still prone to the occasional bucking fit if you tried to make him do dressage for too long – Issie decided it was a good time for him to be retired.

Straight after they took the gold medal she put the stallion on a flight back to New Zealand. Avery had met the horse at the airport and after quarantine Storm had settled into a peaceful retirement at Winterflood Farm.

Knowing that he would be bored to tears if he was stuck in the paddock all day, Issie asked Francoise to ride him for her.

"He remains your horse, of course," Francoise would tell Issie whenever she phoned up from The Laurels to check on him. "I am keeping the saddle warm for you, but Storm is very loyal. He never forgets who his true owner is; I can tell that in his heart he misses you as much as he did when he was a homesick colt in Spain."

Issie felt the same way about Storm. She had ridden so many brilliant, talented horses over the years – and she had great hopes for the future with Mystic. But through it all, she had always felt that Storm was *the one*.

And so, six months after she retired him, she had made the trip back to Chevalier Point. It was a flying visit – just a few days to spare between international events. As she sat down and ate her scrambled eggs, she found herself itching to get to the farm, wanting, as always, to be with her horse.

It had been a long time since Issie had been to the farm, but these days the front gate was hard to miss. A sign had been hung at the entrance with the words *Winterflood Farm* crafted in wrought iron.

As Issie eased her mother's hatchback up the driveway, she couldn't believe how grand this place had become. The little saplings that had once stood on either side of the road had become tall, spreading plane trees and the cottage at the end of the drive had been remodelled to accommodate the family – two children, Xavier, aged ten, and six-year-old Marie-Claude.

Francoise was in the kitchen making crêpes when Issie arrived, and Xavier and Marie-Claude both rushed out as soon as they saw her.

"Issie!" Marie-Claude flung her arms around Issie's waist. "We've got a performance! Mum said we can show you!"

Francoise shrugged apologetically. "I'm sorry, Issie. They have been waiting all morning for you. They're desperate to show you their trick. I hope you don't mind?"

Issie smiled at Marie-Claude. "Come on then – let's go!"

In the paddock directly behind the house, Xavier, the spitting image of his father, busied himself preparing the series of obstacles around the paddock while Marie-Claude went to the stables to get her pony.

A moment later there was the clip-clop of hooves across the concrete of the yard and Marie-Claude returned leading a liver chestnut mare, a pretty Anglo-Arab with a white blaze, a flaxen mane and four white socks.

Issie's heart raced. "Hello, Blaze!" She stroked the mare's velvet-soft muzzle. "What on earth have these two roped you into?"

Blaze was now in her twenties, but the mare was still a beauty. At Winterflood Farm she led the sweet life of the spoilt family pony – her belly was well-rounded and her coat shone like burnished copper.

Both of the children had learnt to ride on her, but now the mare belonged only to Marie-Claude. "They adore each other," Francoise told Issie. "They spend hours together out here. I have no idea what they are up to – one day I came out and found them both lying down underneath that tree over there. Blaze was on her side on the grass and Marie-Claude was snuggled up between her front legs with her head on Blaze's shoulder!"

Marie-Claude clambered on to Blaze with no saddle or bridle. She sat up and wrapped her hands in Blaze's mane and gave her brother the signal. Xavier stood in the centre of the paddock on top of an old wooden crate, acting the ringmaster and calling out instructions as Marie-Claude rode Blaze through the obstacle course. They wound their way through traffic cones and stepped over tarpaulins and logs, then squeezed between oil drums. The finale of the act was the grand moment when Xavier held his hands over his head and Blaze rose up on her hind legs in a perfect rear, with Marie-Claude giggling as she clung on in mid-air.

As Francoise and Issie applauded, Blaze dropped down on to one knee and did a graceful bow.

"You know, that was one of the first tricks I ever taught her," Francoise said wistfully. "She was the best mare in El Caballo Danza Magnifico."

"I know," Issie said. "I remember."

Issie left the children and Francoise in the paddock with Blaze and headed into the stables. There was a time when she thought this place was so vast, but now it felt so tiny.

She found Avery in the old tack shed where the photos of his great horses, including The Soothsayer, still decorated the walls.

"I've got Storm all tacked up for you," her old trainer told her. "He's in the last loose box."

Issie followed him back out into the yard and down to the last box. The top of the Dutch door was left open, and as she got closer Storm heard her footsteps outside and stuck his head out. When he caught sight of Issie he gave a vigorous whinny. Issie laughed.

"Hey, boy! Yes, it's me."

Issie stepped inside the stable and Storm sniffed, checking her out with his nostrils wide and then nickering warmly as if to say, "You're back! Where have you been!"

Issie hugged her horse. "I know. I missed you too."

She led Storm out into the yard and Avery gave her a leg up.

"Francoise and I will have lunch ready when you come back." Avery smiled up at Issie.

"It's nice to see you back up on him," he said. "You always looked so right on that horse."

It was the perfect day for a hack. The weather was clear and sunny, and Storm's deep bay coat shone in the sunlight. Even though he was no longer competing, the stallion looked as fit as he'd ever been. Issie harboured a secret suspicion that if she wanted to, she could have set off at a gallop and aimed him for the River Paddock fence to clear it with ease.

She resisted the urge; Storm had earnt his retirement. The most they would do today was a gentle canter along the grass verges.

At the gates of the River Paddock they halted and Issie looked out over the fields. She didn't recognise any of the ponies in these pastures now.

This had been the place where Issie grazed her horses when she was a pony-club kid. Blaze had lived here. Fortune too, for a little while. And Mystic of course. Dear Mystic. She had never seen him again after that night when the grey colt had been born at The Laurels. She had never expected to, she supposed, but as she looked out over the paddocks and focused her gaze on The Pines, at the far end of the field, she felt her heart beat a little faster. Perhaps the shadows beneath the trees might be hiding a swaybacked grey pony? Would she catch a glimpse once more of his dapples shimmering in the morning sunlight?

Issie stood there for a while longer but the trees didn't hold any secrets any more. With a reluctant last look over her shoulder she rode on.

The backroads were quieter than usual that day. Nightstorm was in a good mood, and as they walked along on a loose rein his merry, snorty grunts seemed to sound like he was humming a tune to himself.

By the time they reached the pony-club grounds, both of them had worked up a bit of a sweat and Issie tied Storm up to the club railing. The club rooms were unlocked and she'd brought enough loose change in her pockets to get a drink from the Coke machine.

Stepping inside the club rooms was like stepping into history. The place was still furnished with the same old overstuffed chairs, all still falling apart. In fact, Issie was pretty sure that those were the same ancient copies of *PONY Magazine* in the basket next to the coffee table.

She put her money in the slot and the drinks machine yielded up a can of Coke. She drank it as she led Storm to the trough and let him have some water. Then it was time to turn around and head home.

The walk back seemed shorter somehow – as they

always do. Issie had just reached the grass verge that ran down the stretch of road from the River Paddock to Winterflood Farm when she heard hoofbeats behind her. She turned around and saw another horse and rider. The horse was a big chestnut, and even though he was clearly out for a casual hack, his rider had a very Natasha Tucker-ish attitude to turnout and had him kitted out in sparkling white boots and a white saddle pad, the sort of tack that Issie kept for best. His rider was also dressed in a tailored jacket and white show jods. They made a stark contrast to Storm, who had a tatty old navy rug under his saddle and Issie whose outfit consisted of a faded old red T-shirt and her oldest, most worn-out beige jods.

The woman cast an eye over Nightstorm. You could see by her expression that she was far from impressed by this slightly tubby and elderly bay hack. She would have given him a wide berth but it was hard to do this without being obviously snobby and so she reluctantly fell in alongside Issie, walking her chestnut at a brisk clip.

"Hi!" Issie said brightly. "Isn't it a super day for a ride?"

"I hack Vanguard out once a week regardless of the weather," the woman replied drily. "It's a vital part of his schooling."

Now that they were side by side, Issie could see that the chestnut horse, Vanguard, totally suited his owner. He had a piggy eye and his ears were permanently flattened back against his head. He clearly didn't fancy having Issie and Storm for company any more than his snooty rider did.

"Do you compete him?" Issie asked, trying to break the ice.

"Of course!" The woman seemed to regard the question as an insult. "Vanguard is a very valuable horse. A hugely experienced eventer! I mean, you're probably not aware of how the eventing world works, but it's a very difficult sport. I've ridden him at several three-days, competing over one-star courses. Massive jumps! Dressage is our forte. I've had lessons from all the best instructors – Germans mostly. None of the local instructors are good enough for me..."

Issie listened as the woman went into a lengthy description of her training regime and every rosette and ribbon that Vanguard had ever won. It was like being back at pony club and being cornered by Natasha Tucker!

It wasn't until they were at the gates of Winterflood Farm, that the woman finally paused for breath. She gave a dismissive glance at the bay horse that she had been riding beside this whole time and said loftily. "So what about him? Has he ever done anything?"

Issie reached down and gave her horse a slappy pat on his neck. "He used to compete," she said, "but he's retired now."

Issie smiled warmly at the woman. "Well, this is where I turn off. Enjoy the rest of your ride. It was nice to meet you."

The woman frowned – they were at the gates of the famous Winterflood Farm. What business could this girl have turning off down there? Ohmygod! It couldn't be! Had she just made a terrible fool of herself?

"Wait!" she called anxiously after the girl. "You didn't tell me your name."

The girl on the bay horse turned back and smiled. "I'm Isadora Brown," she said. "And this is Nightstorm."

Don't miss another amazing series by Stacy Gregg…

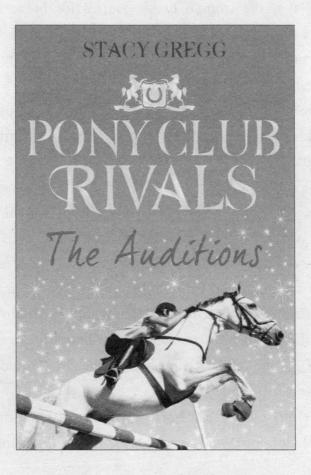

Georgie Parker has to ace the auditions for Blainford
'All-Stars' Academy, only the best riders win places
at this elite international boarding school.

It's an exciting world full of glamour and danger –
and Georgie is determined to live the dream!

PONY CLUB
RIVALS

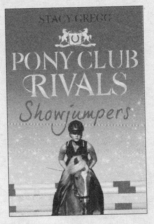

Read them all!

Every girl dreams of becoming a princess.
But this real-life princess has a dream of her own.

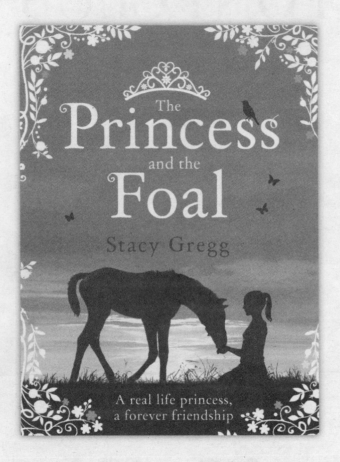

Discover the incredible story
of Princess Haya and her foal.

Two girls are divided by time, united by their love
for some very special horses, in this epic
Caribbean adventure.

The
Island of
Lost Horses

Stacy Gregg

A real life mystery,
an incredible friendship

Based on the extraordinary true story of the Abaco Barb,
a real life mystery that has remained unsolved
for over five hundred years.

Stacy Gregg

The Girl Who Rode the Wind

Her bond with one horse
will echo through the ages…

An epic, emotional story of two girls and their bond
with beloved horses, set in Italy during the
Second World War and the present day.

One family's history of adventure and heartbreak –
and how it is tied to the world's most dangerous
horse race, the Palio.